ALSO BY A

THE FREED HUNT

FORGED IN FLAMES

VALUE IN VISIONS (out 14th August 2022)

SOFTEST KINKSTERS

THE SOFTEST KINKSTERS COLLECTION

THE HIMBO LIBRARIAN COLLECTION (out 14th November 2022)

FORGED IN FLAMES

ALI WILLIAMS

Forged in Flames
Published by Claficionado Press Ltd

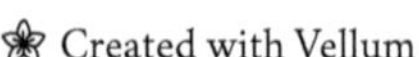
Created with Vellum

NEWSLETTER

Do you want to find out more about my books and romance lectures? Join my mailing list and be the first to find out my next releases!

AliWilliams.org/Contact

Ali Williams

AUTHOR, EDITOR, ACADEMIC

AUTHOR NOTE

Please be aware that *Forged in Flames* includes explicit sex, including worship kink, cunnilingus, blowjobs, and some very enthusiastic shagging. It also contains references to PTSD, trauma, violence (mainly off-page, and some nonexplicit on-page) and death (off-page). I hope I have treated these issues with the care they and you deserve.

DEDICATION

This one is for me.
Because I didn't know if I could.

CONTENTS

1

⚒⚒⚒

SPARKS flew across the forge as Kenna brought the hammer down against the steel again and again, pounding the metal into waves of fire that seemed to undulate by the light of the furnace. Grasping the sheet with her tongs, she turned to plunge the piece into water. Steam hissed as soon as it hit the liquid, the dampness in the air making the strands of hair cling to the nape of her neck. She grinned. It was time to pull it out and lay the newly quenched piece carefully back on the anvil.

Gorgeous.

This really was the best way to start her day, allowing the thrill of the pure physicality of forging to take hold so she could lose herself to the heat and the flames. To really connect with the metal and the fire and that all-consuming heat that got underneath her skin until she just *had* to fire up the furnace to let it out.

Definitely far more satisfying than having to consider projects that just weren't quite right.

Her steel-capped boots thudded as she moved across the forge to look at the sculpture again. Her current project had called for a lot of consideration. For a lot of stopping and looking. Thinking. Planning.

There was something very satisfying about working in both steel and bronze, a melding of casting and forging that took her back to her days at university, where she got to experiment with all kinds of metalwork. And there was a warmth present in the bronze that definitely suited the naked curves of the woman before her. A female figure rising from flames towards... Towards what, she wasn't quite sure.

And therein lay her problem with this piece. Aesthetically it was pretty damn gorgeous, even if she thought so herself, but the sculpture felt like it was missing something. Unlike most of her work—archways and structures that slotted into the landscape of the South Downs—this was for a private collector, one who'd said they wanted a sculpted figure and left the rest of the details to her. For most artists, it'd be a bit of a dream, having the freedom to do whatever they wanted, but Kenna's work was all about function and place and specificity. What was the point of spending hours bent over the anvil, working the power hammer or doing delicate casting work in temperatures that would make the most hardened of smiths melt, if the end product didn't fit into the space it was meant for?

Besides, the process of creating something for a private collection was different from what she usually did. Most of her art was focused on the space where she'd created it, the tiny village of Tunford, slap bang in the middle of one of the UK's most beautiful national parks. A place where the most exciting event in the calendar was the annual cricket match—and only then because of the year the headteacher of the primary school fell in the pond. And past the village? Just rolling hills as far as the eye could see. Everything she usually created ended up becoming part of this wider community: the railings round the village pond (clearly needed postpondgate), the sign for the local pub, and pieces that had function for local agriculture.

Admittedly, her grant had helped her afford to focus on those types of pieces. She'd had to fight for the funding, to prove herself in an industry where being a woman didn't exactly make things easy, but her work spoke for itself. Unfortunately, grants like those were few and far between, and this commission would more than pay for a couple of months of materials and the upkeep of the forge. She couldn't grumble, especially when she secretly relished playing the silent and tortured artist for investors who just didn't know any better. And this investor had named a price she couldn't really afford to turn down and allowed her to make whatever she wanted.

After she'd told her friends Rina and Arlee, they had spent the rest of the weekend celebrating at the Golden Martlet, playing darts and pool and generally toasting to her first private commission. But as the three of them had headed out of the pub together, she had absolutely no idea what she was going to make.

Kenna wasn't entirely certain where the eventual idea came from—leftover remnants from a dream she couldn't quite remember perhaps—but the woman in the sculpture had leapt unbidden into her work like she'd been waiting to be seen for far too long.

The flames surrounding the figure? Those had been Kenna's own private rebellion; forged from steel, hammered on the anvil, and smoothed and shined until they almost seemed alive. They were her favourite part of the piece.

She ran her hand across the flames. The reflection of bronze and the steel looked as if they were setting the woman aflame, making her a phoenix in human form, rising from fire.

But for all that, the piece still needed soul.

She sighed and moved impatiently forward, meeting the metal gaze with her own. "What is it that you need, lady? Well? Tell me so I can be done with you."

It had been a long couple of months working on a piece with no real clue of where she was going, or how she'd feel when she finally got there, and something in her was ready to snap. The culmination of all her efforts was just out of reach.

The hard line of her mouth softened, and for a moment she could have sworn there was something akin to compassion in the eyes that she'd crafted in bronze. Something almost tender.

She laughed abruptly. This was why Rina and Arlee said she needed a break. They were used to the Kenna with a slight swagger to her step, not someone who talked to metal figures and imagined the face was looking back at her. At this stage in the project, she wasn't even sure that she recognised herself. Something about her need to finish this commission just felt…off.

This was more than her usual impatience to see the finished piece; there was a deep-seated longing that was more than a little unsettling, and Kenna was quite certain she'd never felt anything quite like this *compulsion* before.

Leaning in, she gently blew away some shavings on the figure's thigh, pausing in irritation when she realised it was in fact a blemish that would need some hard work and more than a little elbow grease to polish it out. She ran her thumb over it, gauging the depth and width of the mark, only to startle when the steel gave way to flesh.

✦✦✦

BELISAMA LOOKED DOWN TO WHERE THE MORTAL'S HAND rested on her thigh and raised an eyebrow. The poor thing seemed fairly taken aback, although she supposed it had been more than a few centuries since she'd last visited a forge in person. And mortals did startle ever so easily. She'd need to be a little understanding.

"Dear mortal—"

"What the fuck?!"

She paused, furrowing her brow. She recognised the language from years behind the Veil, watching mortals' lives as if they were a play, but it was hardly appropriate for it to be used in her presence.

"I beg your pardon?"

But the redhead had backed away from her, wide-eyed, and seemed to be muttering something about long hours and psychosis and the need for vodka. Clearly her new priestess needed a few moments to adjust. Belisama sat, pulling the flames about her. They wouldn't keep their shape for long, but they didn't exactly need to. And a flaming robe was always such a great look.

She watched as the mortal walked determinedly over, rubbed her eyes, and looked again.

"Dear mortal—"

"Kenna."

"Stop interrupting me!" The flames flared a little, but the mortal seemed undeterred.

"Listen. It's Kenna. Not mortal. This…this dream or whatever the hell it is, is mine. And I'll do what I bloody well like."

The mortal—Kenna—reached out and swore again as the flames burnt her hand. Belisama saw a flicker of real terror cross the woman's face. She was fairly certain that her new priestess now knew she wasn't dreaming. There was a thud as Kenna pulled away and sat solidly on the table behind her.

"Are you ready to listen now?"

One quiet nod.

"I am Belisama, Goddess of the Forge and Fire, of Crafts and Light, and you are my priestess."

The mortal's eyes widened and, before she could open her mouth, Belisama hurriedly added, "Not a virgin priestess, I assure you. I'm not Vesta." She resisted the urge to add something very rude about Roman Goddesses and their apparent fear of a healthy orgasm. It probably wasn't the right time. Priestess to induct and all that.

"No offence, your Goddessness—"

She quite liked that actually. She'd have to mention it to Andraste.

"—but I don't think I've ever actually heard of you before."

Belisama stopped.

Once, every person in Britain had known of her, of her skill and craft, and had petitioned for aid in the forge. And now? Here was a smith who not only didn't worship her, but had never even heard of her.

After the Menai Massacre she'd refused to be amalgamated with a Roman counterpart, unlike so many of her fellow Briton Gods and Goddesses. Poor Sulis had become Sulis-Minerva, forever remembered as the Briton Goddess who was just a facet of someone else. It was a fate Belisama had refused to bow to. Instead, she'd been trapped behind the Veil that had been drawn across this world, watching as the centuries rolled by and her true home, the forge, almost fell out of existence. She'd been forced to watch generation after generation be born, grow old, and die, always just out of reach from those she could have helped, from those who could have saved her with their worship. And this was the result.

"I…" How did she explain that? Explain centuries of grief and loss for who she'd been, to a mortal who'd barely lived a few decades on the earth?

She settled for the basic truth. "I'm a Briton. You'd consider me pre-Roman."

Kenna quirked her head to one side. "Pre-Roman…"

"Yes."

"A pre-Roman goddess."

"Exactly."

"A pre-Roman goddess, who thinks that I'm her priestess. Right. Cos that makes all of the sense."

She sighed impatiently. "I don't think *you're my priestess; you* are *my priestess. You've spent the last few months working in clay, casting and then forging to create a statue of me."*

"Huh."

"You're what we'd call Godstouched. Blessed with skill beyond your ken."

"My skill…? Do you mean in the forge?"

She inclined her head. To be honest, she was fairly impressed with how well this Kenna had taken the news. There'd been significantly less screaming and fainting than she was used to, although also a distinct lack of prostration and declaration of unworthiness. She got the impression that the latter wasn't going to happen any time soon. And just as well really, because prostrate priests and priestesses had a habit of being too meek to stand the flames of her ministry.

"Besides," she added, "It was you who breathed me into the statue."

"My breath?" *Belisama watched as Kenna breathed onto her hand. Nothing.*

"Your powers will grow with time."

"My powers. Right."

"You doubt me?" The flames flared once more against her skin.

"Look, it's like this." *The mortal met her eyes, straight on. That hadn't happened for millennia.* "Let's say, for the sake of argument, that this is all real. I don't have the time to be a priestess. You've just destroyed my latest commission—took months to make, by the way—and I'm going to need to get straight onto making something new before I have to return my advance. Which I can't afford to do."

"Your commission?"

"The sculpture you've just, I don't know, embodied? Taken over? Possessed?"

"It will be unharmed." Belisama shook off the flames and stood, towering above her new priestess. "All I ask is a commission for me. Fully forged in flames—no casting. And," she added, before the redhead could interrupt again, "I will bestow upon you the blessing of my patronage. Your breath will be imbued with flames, your mind free to soar, and the sky will embrace you. But make me the sun. I am the Goddess of Light, after all."

She exhaled gently, suffusing the air with her own power, and watched with satisfaction as the mortal breathed it in.

Reluctant inductee to the priestesshood Kenna might be, but channelling such power meant that Belisama would get her commission, one way or another. Fighting such gifts never ended very well for mortals.

⚒⚒⚒

"THE SUN. RIGHT. ANYTHING ELSE? DO YOU WANT ME TO pull the moon from the sky as well?"

Silence.

Kenna blinked several times in succession and then looked hard at the sculpture, which now looked identical to how it had when she'd first entered the forge that morning. "I seriously need some coffee," she muttered. "Clearly I've been working way too hard. Goddesses and priestesses and breath imbued with flames indeed."

She jumped down from the table and headed straight to the only altar in the building, where her office kettle sat. Two minutes later, she had a steaming mug of instant coffee, the kind that made Rina shudder and Arlee bemoan the ways of the world. One sip and she sighed. She'd mainline the stuff if she could.

Absentmindedly, she ran her thumb over the small welt forming on the back of her hand. A burn. *Nope. Nuh-uh.* She took another sip hurriedly. That must have been from her session on the anvil yesterday, not from some forged steel bursting into actual flames.

But the coffee didn't settle her the way that it usually did; instead, her stomach felt distinctly unsettled. Kenna hiccupped, the sensation rising like a weird heat, and then she looked in disbelief at the result.

There were flames in her mug.

She closed her eyes, counted ten and then to twenty just in case, before opening them again. The flames were still very much there and, even worse, she could feel a second hiccup following the first.

"Fuck."

2

THE dirt beneath his hands was harsh, chafing against his skin after the soft suppleness of the leather reins he'd held for centuries. Morcant clutched at the ground desperately, unwilling to believe that it was real. That this was real.

For too long he'd imagined a moment like this. When he'd be able to dismount from his horse without crumbling into dust. Without joining his brother in oblivion.

And now? Now he was on the ground, touching the earth he thought he'd never feel again. Breathing air as a free man for the first time in millennia.

The wind cut across the Downs and sliced at his face, and now he truly felt it. His skin and clothes were buffeted and battered; each gust coaxed fear and pain from him. His eyes, streaming in the cold he hadn't felt for thousands of years.

They'd been freed from the Wild Hunt.

He'd forgotten it could feel like this, standing on the earth, experiencing the weather's tempestuous tantrums. In some ways he hoped, nay *prayed*, that he was dreaming, because if they'd been given a taste of freedom only to have it snatched away... The idea of having to mount his horse once more, and ready himself to watch the world spin by, watching lives beginning and ending again and again and again... He took a deep breath. He wasn't dreaming, and so, if he truly had been given a chance to walk the earth once more, he wouldn't waste it. He'd walk for hours just to feel the wind in his hair. He'd stand in the rain. And he'd bask in the warmth of the sun. No more colourless hinterland, sensation-less, where nothing ever changed.

It had been hard, harder than any of them liked to admit at this stage, watching the world go by without them. Ages rising and falling in the blink of an eye, and technological advances in recent years that made his head hurt just thinking about them. Almost as though the world had been spinning too fast for him to keep up. Trapped in the Hunt, behind the Veil, they'd stagnated. Always just beyond the reach of the mortals whose lives they could see. Lives they could never engage with.

This had been their life for centuries: remnants of a twenty-strong party who'd gone into the Otherworld for a wedding and returned cursed by the Gods, damned to ride the Wild Hunt for all eternity. At first, the idea of being a hunting party made sense—a function they understood at least—but then they realised they were chasing after nothing. There was no one to hunt down, no animal to chase. The entire Hunt was merely a means to enhance Nodens' power.

Morcant stopped that train of thought immediately. Just thinking the God of Hunting's name had brought him hither previously, and the last thing Morcant wanted right now was for this peace and quiet to be disrupted by his brash ego. Besides, the sooner the god realised they were free, the sooner they were destined to return to the Hunt. The longer he was able to put off that return, the better. The five of them deserved that at least.

He looked towards the other, similarly disorientated figures. Deuroc looked truly sombre for the first time in decades. There was something jarring about seeing his face absent of his usual smile, and Morcant quickly turned away, looking for his king instead.

Herla had been the greatest of the Kings of the Britons, a proud and strong leader of tribes. Now, he sat silent, a shadow of the king he'd once been, staring at the bloodhound that'd been their unknowing captor for all that time. The animal trotted to Herla and licked his face, and the laugh that broke from the man was hoarse and bitter. When they'd left the Otherworld, they'd been warned not to dismount until the bloodhound jumped down from his spot on Herla's saddle. Those who had ignored the warning had dissipated the moment their feet touched the ground.

Dissipated into nothingness as if they'd never existed in the first place.

But a dog is a dog, no matter how much resentment they felt towards it, and centuries of holding him in his lap had softened Herla's approach to their unwitting captor. In fact, they all cherished the Hound, as they'd come to call him, the dog being the only source of true unwavering affection they'd received over the years. He ate the meat they fed him, made little gruffly noises when scratched just so behind those floppy ears, and had loved each of them with a passion reserved for man's best friend. They'd hated and loved him in equal measure and now, when he was no longer unknowingly trapping them, he was just a dog.

Morcant watched as the Hound softly padded over to Sten, nudging his hand until the Dane ran it gently over his head. Sten had spoken only a little over the centuries but even he had doted upon the dog. There'd been a connection between them that had resulted in whines and whimpering from the Hound whenever Sten had ridden too far ahead of the rest of them.

For Sten, this freedom must feel bittersweet. He was still stuck in Britain, hundreds of miles from his true home, Scandinavia. He'd followed his jarl across the sea, fought alongside him, and then buried his fellow warriors amongst the sapling yew trees that now dwarfed their burial mounds. The Hunt had caught him, a lone survivor whose purpose had been to live and die with his comrades, even further from home than the rest of them. Nodens's trick had trapped Sten in more ways than one.

Aerten, on the other hand, had opted for this life. There'd been no women in their original group, but the warrior woman who'd joined their ranks, streaks of battle woad still adorning her face, was unequivocally one of them.

They'd offered her and her sister the protection of the Hunt after the defeat of their mother, Boudica. He and Deuroc and Herla had trawled the battlefield for hours, looking for survivors amongst the eighty thousand dead, and had fallen across the barely alive sisters. Brianne was no longer of the Hunt, but Aerten was. She'd chosen to join them, persuaded her sister to leave their grief behind and had mounted her horse with no fear and no regrets. She was the only one of them who now stood, looking out across the hills of the South Downs.

They were, he realised, at the very pinnacle of Cissbury Ring, an old hillfort that had once been strewn with farmers and settlers. Now abandoned, deathly quiet in the morning air, it had become the site of their freedom. It seemed quite fitting that they returned to life where so much life had once thrived.

He sat on his haunches and looked over the rolling hills, breathing in air tinged with salt from the ocean, a mere half-hour's ride away. He was relieved to note their horses were grazing quietly beside them. Riding was one thing he didn't want to give up to freedom, especially as the alternative was a car. He'd seen the filthy things from their inception to their conquest of the land, and he'd be damned if he rode inside one of those contraptions.

"Morcant."

That voice.

He closed his eyes, and desperately tried to sear each sensation that surrounded him into his memories. The earthy smell of the grass. Air cold against his skin. That salt in the air against his tongue. Each recorded, filed away. Each captured for when they'd be lost, tucked out of reach beyond the Veil.

"Morcant."

More insistent now. He stood, unwilling, to where Nodens stood behind him.

"Oh God of the Hunt. God of Dogs. God of the Sea and of Healing." His voice was harsh, angry even. Just having to say the word hunt, when he knew he'd be sent back there all too soon, seemed cruel.

"Why, Morcant, you don't seem too pleased to see me. Shouldn't you be praising my name for freeing you all?"

There were many things he hated about Nodens. The insincerity of his words; the joy he clearly took in tormenting them; the expected worship from those he'd imprisoned. But then there was the fact that Morcant was the only one he appeared to. That was the hardest of all. He was the one who had to tell everyone else every time the god had some passing fancy, or a message, or some cruel jibe that he insisted Morcant communicate to the rest of the Hunt.

Once, he'd have considered himself blessed to be Godstouched, but after centuries of this low-level shit, he knew better.

"You freed us?" He knew he sounded incredulous, but

what else could be expected, especially after centuries of their pleas falling on deaf ears?

"I did indeed." Nodens preened a little and then scowled when he realised that Morcant wasn't overly impressed. *"Really? This is your response? Where's the appreciation? The gratitude for my benevolence?"*

Morcant leaned back, grounding his hands in the grass, soil embedding itself beneath his fingernails. The feel of it emboldened him, and all of a sudden, he found himself furious. "You've never done anything without a reason before, so why start now?"

"In mistaking my actions for leniency, you forget yourself. Surely you remember what happened to your companions who questioned me. Who doubted me. Think of your brother."

There was a strange shimmering around the god's figure, resulting in the sort of pressure at the back of Morcant's eyes that you'd usually get from staring too long at the sun. It hurt. A lot. That's what he got for challenging a god, he supposed.

"You will do what I need. And then, if you complete the task to my satisfaction, the Wild Hunt will remain freed."

He raised an eyebrow. Possibly unwise, considering how his head was currently aching, but there was something about Nodens that invited insolence. "You'll need to let me know what it is then."

"There's another Godstouched, a woman, whose patron would destroy everything I've built. Stop her."

"Stop her from what? What is she doing?"

The glow he faced this time was almost overwhelming. *"Questions, questions, questions. Always questions. Can't you just do as you're directed?"*

Morcant got the distinct impression that Nodens didn't quite know who or what he was looking for, which frankly seemed to add some reason to the god's usual unpredictability. Trying to rationalise his behaviour was probably an act of foolishness in itself, but freedom at so small a price just didn't seem right, and trusting in the Gods had resulted in the Hunt in the first place.

"Is there nothing else that you could—"

"You have the Sage," the god bellowed.

This was true. At first appearances, Deuroc seemed the least sage-like of men, but he had been the one to find Aerten and Brianne on the battlefield, and it was he who always knew when Morcant had been speaking to Nodens. Finding a Godstouched woman in a time when the Godstouched were few and far between seemed like a fairly achievable goal.

Morcant forced himself to meet the god's gaze, shuddering when the feeling of unworthiness and insignificance enveloped him like a fog. It was, however, one of the few rebellious moves he'd had in his arsenal whilst stuck on a horse.

"I could say no."

"You like being a part of the Wild Hunt? I could rename it. From Herlaþing to Morca—"

"Fine." Morcant's hands tightened and then loosened, torn grass falling from his palms. He'd seen what leading the hunt had done to Herla; the guilt that hounded him every day. "I'll do it."

"There was never truly a question of you doing otherwise."

He blurted out the next question, not wanting to face more of the god's ire but needing to hear the answer. "And the whole Hunt will be freed? All of us?"

"All of you. Just stop the Godstouched."

And then he disappeared, the pain splitting Morcant's head in two instantly vanishing. A pile of folded clothing appeared beside him which he paid scant attention to.

For the first time since he'd hit the ground and felt the

earth beneath his hands, Morcant actually felt like he had something propelling him forward. He had an aim, a goal to head towards, and he couldn't think of any more important. The question of what he'd do with the promised newfound freedom could be put aside for the time being.

Because he had a quest.

3

⚒⚒⚒

"FUCKITY fuck."

So it turned out that having hiccups after having been visited by an ancient goddess, meant that you were likely to melt the Tupperware container that you left on the side of the table. The one with your lunch in it. It served her right, really, for not putting it straight into the fridge when she got in. That would be little consolation later when she got hungry, but Kenna had a feeling that hiccupping flames all over the place was going to have serious consequences for her appetite.

Twenty minutes in and they were showing no signs of disappearing, and God—Goddess, she supposed—knew that she'd tried pretty much everything. Downing a glass of water as fast as possible? Teeny flames shot out her nose. And gargling with saltwater had only resulted in it evaporating in a mist that steamed up the entire office and frosted the window with salt crystals.

In fact, she'd skedaddled out of the room pretty darn quick after trying to hold her breath to get rid of the damn things, but instead, scorched an innocent pile of paperwork. There was now a smouldering pile of ashes where her printed invoices had been. In theory, she should probably feel some kind of regret, but it had been particularly satisfying to see the bill for the casting of Belisama's figure go up in smoke, especially considering the trouble the goddess had brought with her.

Goddess. Now that really was a turn-up for the books. Kenna wasn't what anyone would really call a believer in the divine, but you couldn't argue with the burn on her hand and the path of destruction left in the wake of fiery hiccups. Besides, she'd pinched herself so many times that the back of her hand ached; this was clearly no dream.

She hiccupped again and winced as the flames hit the side of her power hammer. The tools in the forge were fairly robust, of that she was certain, but she needed to find a solution for these fucking hiccups before she accidentally heated a piece of work. The forged flames would probably stand up to the heat, but she didn't want to risk the cast bronze or the smaller steel pieces that she'd been playing with earlier in the week.

Besides, what she really needed after the surreal events of the morning was a trip to the pub, and she highly doubted that Tegan would be overly delighted if she singed the new paintwork or ruined the varnish of the bar. Though, to be fair, she could set her own flaming sambuca on fire. That party trick would have to be worth something.

She glanced at the clock on the wall. Nine. In the morning. Definitely far too early to even be considering booze.

Another hiccup.

It took a lot to get Kenna down. She'd continued on when her father had passed, and she hadn't even blinked when the arts funding she'd been receiving hadn't been renewed earlier this year. But this? Talking statues and goddesses and being told she was a priestess and hiccupping flames and not being able to leave her forge due to the kind of nightmarish shit that didn't even crop up in nightmares because it was too freaking out there? This was starting to get her down.

Fuck it.

She might as well put her hiccups to good use.

Striding to her workbench, she picked up a piece of copper and then moved to her anvil. This time when the flames hit, she aimed them at the copper, watching carefully to not over-heat them. As the hiccups slowed, and with them the turmoil in her stomach, that all-familiar glow remained across the heated metal. She grinned and reached for her hammer.

This was going to be fun.

SHE MUST HAVE BEEN FORGING FOR A COUPLE OF HOURS WHEN she heard knocking on the door. Stepping back, she looked around. The different pieces of copper she'd been working on resembled something akin to a ray of light. Kenna wasn't entirely certain when her hiccups had dissipated, but she thought that it might have something to do with the fact that she now seemed to wield some kind of control over them.

The knocking turned to thumping. Possibly even pounding, by the sound of it. Whoever it was clearly hadn't read the "Hammering is done in my forge, not on my door" sign that was hanging outside. Definitely not Arlee—primary school teachers didn't ever seem to leave school premises during the week, even if the school was one of those liberal ones that involved children choosing what classes to attend—and her standing weekly lunch-date with Rina wasn't for another couple of days.

She marched over, casually resting her hammer on her

shoulder in a very intentional who-the-hell-is-interrupting-the-smith-with-the-huge-hammer way and slid the door open. "What?"

Muscles. That was her overarching impression. Lots and lots of muscles. The kind of muscles you got from doing actual hard physical work, as opposed to in the gym or on the rugby field.

The man attached to the muscles wasn't one that she recognised, and she knew everyone in Tunford. Hard not to in a village that small. Besides, he looked distinctly tired than any farmer she'd ever seen, even during lambing season, and she knew for certain that she'd never seen shoulders that broad before. He ran a hand roughly through his hair, almost shyly, and she instantly wanted to catch his hand in hers. Either that or run her own equally calloused hand through his roughly shorn hair and make him smile for her. In fact, there were a number of things she could think of that she'd rather like to make him do for her.

"Miss…?" His voice trailed off, and she realised that she'd been staring at him for a smidgeon longer than was actually polite.

"I'm the Smith." Kenna made sure to capitalise the word. Many people saw a woman in a forge and assumed that she was here to have a horse shoed by the actual smith or was some kind of jewellery artisan. She was terrible with horses —damn creatures seemed to always chomp or stomp down on whichever of her appendages were closest to them—and jewellery crafting required the kind of detailed finesse that she'd always felt was wasted about someone's neck.

Luckily, Mr. Tall, Dark, and Broad-Shouldered didn't seem to be one of those assumption-makers.

"I see. So, this is your forge, and I've disturbed you whilst you are working."

"Yes." She met his eyes, a sharp dismissal readying her

lips, only to have them frozen upon her tongue when he smiled sheepishly at her. His smile was as delicious as she'd imagined.

"In that case you have my apologies."

"I'm Kenna," she said, suddenly wanting to know more of the stranger on her doorstep. "And you are…?"

"Morcant." This time his smile was more warm than sheepish, and she couldn't help but smile back at him, replying to him with warmth of her own.

"Well, Morcant." The smile turned to a grin as he flushed deliciously when she said his name. Damn if she didn't want to make him blush all over. "How can I help you?"

She'd never have said it out loud, but there were plenty of things that she could imagine helping him with. Starting with releasing the tension that thrummed through his body; she could only imagine what he'd be like, all relaxed and languid. Kenna gave herself a mental slap. *Bad blacksmith.* The poor man probably just wanted directions or something, not to be made the centre of her X-rated fantasies.

As he opened his mouth to answer, a particularly vicious gust of wind curled through the door of the forge and caught her by surprise, her spluttering cough surprising them both. Well, perhaps it was less the cough, and more the shower of sparks that singed his beard.

Oops.

THE BEST THING ABOUT HAVING YOUR BODY FROZEN WHILST you gallop away the centuries was the fact that haircuts weren't needed. Herla and Sten had flowing locks, but Morcant's beard was short and fairly similar in style to some of the men that he'd seen live and die over the last couple of decades. It also meant that he didn't particularly appreciate it getting singed, no matter if the singe-er had hair to match the sparks that had nearly lit him on fire.

Kenna stood, nonchalant, a rogue wisp of smoke curling out from under her top lip the only indication of the sparks' origin.

"Huh." He wasn't often struck for words, but whatever he had imagined when Nodens had pointed him in the direction of the Godstouched, it certainly hadn't been this. Or, indeed, her. Kenna. Red-haired and defiant, hammer in one hand, the other placed on her hip. It took everything in him not to fall to his knees and beg to worship her.

"What?"

"Sparks just came out of your mouth."

"Oh, you noticed that."

Of course he'd noticed; she'd nearly set his beard on fire. "Yes. Surprisingly enough, I *did* notice the sparks coming out of your mouth."

She paused at his words, head tilted, "You're not…scared? Confused? About to run screaming from my door?"

"I'm surprised," he offered up. "But no. I'm not scared."

She swung the hammer down, catching the head in her hand and weighting it thoughtfully. He tried to keep breathing steadily, but good grief the woman was powerful. Strong. Possibly stronger than he. His brain almost shorted out as he imagined her putting all that strength to use on him.

"Okay then. That's not exactly normal, and I know," she continued before he could interrupt, "that the whole sparks-flying-out-of-mouth thing isn't exactly normal either. But if you're less thrown by this turn of events than I am, you might as well come in and tell me just who the hell you are, man-who-breathing-fire-doesn't-phase."

She gestured towards the forge and then, just as he was

about to move past her, rested her hammer against his chest. "And don't think that I'm helpless. I make my living forging and pounding metal, so just try me."

Morcant met her forthright look and nodded silently, fighting the urge to fix his eyes on where the bulge of her bicep curved beneath her sleeve. He'd fought alongside warrior women before—he'd ridden with Aerten for the best part of two millennia – but here was a woman completely at home in her own strength in a different kind of way. Owning her position of authority as the Smith. It was intoxicating, and he wanted it to be her against his chest. Warm skin, not the metal of a hammer, feeling the thud of his heart.

When she took a step back, he almost followed, unthinkingly drawn to her, before forcing himself to move past her into the forge itself.

There was more light in Kenna's forge than in those that he remembered from his era. The anvil more polished and precisely shaped, a huge contraption that looked like an oversized version of the hammer that she held, and a furnace that seemed oddly empty.

His gaze fell upon the table of copper, each piece freshly quenched and shining brightly, and then to the bronze statue in the corner. This time, his feet moved without him thinking, fast and panicked, to where it loomed up out of steel flames.

The statue was unlike anything he'd ever seen before, the stone figurines that his people fashioned of the Gods deliberately vague, without defined features. Anyone with any sense would know not to encourage *their* attention like this, but in this age where technology and media were worshipped like gods in their own right, who would know to keep humans from making mistakes like these?

Yes, the Romans had been keen on huge, life-sized figures, but where were they now? Some small, logical part of his brain pointed out that he and the Hunt were all who were left of the Britons, and that not creating images of the Gods hadn't exactly saved them, but he pushed the thought aside. This sculpture. This piece. It was all too much. Too big, too lifelike, too clearly an act of worship.

"Who?"

"I'm sorry?" Kenna's words were deliberately bland, he could tell.

"Who is it? Tell me!" His raised voice didn't echo, the sound deadened and swallowed up by the metal surrounding them.

She shifted the hammer in her hands once more. "If you're going to shout, then you can leave."

Morcant stopped, made motionless by the look of caution in her eyes. "I…I'm sorry. I didn't mean to. But you have to know that what you're doing, deliberately summoning a goddess, puts us all in danger."

"Deliberately—" Her words cut off, and she put the hammer down. Hard. "I didn't deliberately do *anything*. I'm a smith. A sculptor. Deliberately summoning a goddess indeed." She stalked over to him and met his eyes straight on. "I didn't ask for this, and I don't have time for some cocksure prick walking into *my* forge and yelling at me about *my* sculpture."

Morcant couldn't remember the last time he'd been challenged like this, up close. As part of the Hunt, they'd long accepted that arguments resulted in one of them riding ahead or even silent treatment until too many years had passed for it to matter anymore.

Instead, Kenna was so close he could feel her breath batting against his lips as she spoke, each word a veritable hit. He didn't know whether he needed to step away, or to lean into the threat of her anger. Both. Neither.

"And as for who? She's Belisama. She's claimed me as her

priestess, or some such nonsense, and she's the reason why I could probably scorch your eyebrows off if I so wanted, so *back the fuck off.*"

4

⚒⚒⚒

THIS was the problem with letting guys with broad shoulders and calloused hands into her forge. Firstly, he'd distracted her with the whole sheepish aren't-I-adorable-and-I'm-oh-so-sorry-for-interrupting-you smile, then with the kind of frame that made her want to be the one being worked on the anvil for once, and then he'd turned round and hit her with the you-don't-know-what-you're-doing thing.

Okay, so he may well have had a point there, but she didn't need him to spell it out for her. She was far from oblivious to the weirdness of her situation.

Of *course* it was all bound for disaster. She knew that much from what little she remembered from school about the Gods. Admittedly, those were all Greco-Roman myths, but she didn't imagine that Celtic or Briton or whatever the fuck Gods they were, were going to be much different.

And then there was the whole breathing fire thing, which was hardly going to end well. She could bluster all she wanted about scorching Morcant's eyebrows off, but she could actually do it, for Goddess's sake. And yes, she'd already started thinking in female deities. Next thing she knew, she'd be calling out "Goddess, more!" and a literal goddess would pop up when he hit that sweet spot.

Not him. Someone else. Who was most definitely not him.

Because there was no way that he was going to be coming anywhere near her or her orgasms any time soon. That honour had to be earned, and she was very determinedly *not* going to think about the ways in which she'd make him earn it.

She was rather pleased to see, however, that he was looking rattled after her outburst and had taken a step back. But when his eyes dropped to her lips, she rubbed them roughly, set on ignoring the tingle there. That was clearly some kind of after-flame tingle, nothing else.

"You're Belisama's priestess?" His hoarse question cut through her thoughts.

"Yup. Godstouched and everything."

"I know *that*." He still looked frustrated, but also a little chastened. Her getting all up in his space had clearly worked. She'd liked the way that he'd backed down a little, submitting in the face of her authority. Though it was a pity that she couldn't quite keep focused on the whole breathing fire, putting them all in danger thing.

Wait.

"You said that I was putting us all in danger. Who's us?"

He walked over to a chair by the wall then looked at her and raised an eyebrow. She nodded in acquiescence, and he sat.

"The Godstouched are rare, in your time at least," he began. "And I know of no Briton god who's claimed anyone for their priesthood since the age of the Romans. There's been an uneasy balance for centuries, with magic just outside your touch, and now that the Veil is damaged, it's all leaking back in. You have to stop."

The same confusion that had flooded her when Belisama first appeared, happened again. Kenna stood motionless, determined not to show anything on her face whilst she worked this out.

"My time?"

"Yes, I'm—" he paused, and the fury she'd felt at being confronted about her work surged again.

"Don't lie to me."

His eyes met hers, dark timeless windows opening beneath her look. "I'm from the same time as…as *her*." He nodded his head towards the statue. A second pause, and then when he opened his mouth again, a torrent of words flowed out. "I'm of the Wild Hunt, have been for centuries, and now we've been freed. But if the Gods are interfering in mortal lives once more, you don't understand what they can do. How they can change your life. The lives of those you love. Everyone's lives. Whatever you're doing, Kenna, you need to stop. Right now."

She felt like she was drowning in his gaze, being pulled under by the fear there. Kenna wasn't sure whether it was fear for himself, or for her, but she would have sworn to the fact that it was all-encompassing.

He blinked, breaking his hold and she took a large breath. In some ways she was surprised by how calmly she was taking the news that this man, who seemed to tick each and every box of attraction, was centuries old. But, then again, that was probably the least outlandish thing that had been said to her that day.

"What did *she* ask you to do?"

Instinctively, she looked towards the anvil and the rays of

copper light strewn across the nearby work surface, but when he stood, she stepped towards him. "No."

"Kenna..."

"No." Kenna wasn't sure why she was reacting to this so strongly, especially when she'd barely blinked at the Hunt-thing he'd declared moments earlier. Perhaps this was the pinnacle of the longest morning she'd experienced in a while. That made sense. And, to be honest, she'd had about all she could take. This time when she spoke, her words were infused with something she couldn't quite describe, a little like the way that her breath seemed to prickle with heat of flames yet to flare. Those pieces were *hers,* and no one should try to stop her working on them.

He took a step back, falling back into the chair once more, and she felt a surge of *something* at his submission. "They are not yours to touch. And," she added, "they are not hers either. They are mine, and there's no way that someone else is going to disrupt the flow of my work again today."

She strode to where the door of the forge lay gaping, the lush green hills of the Downs just beyond. "Leave, Morcant."

HE STOOD OUTSIDE THE FORGE, THE DOOR SHUT AND (FROM the sounds of it) bolted behind him. The warmth of the midday sun warmed his skin, like her flames had. Her breath had. She had.

And she'd been so angry with him. Like it was his fault and not the goddess's.

Morcant half-turned to knock on the door and then stopped. She didn't want him there. She needed space. And somehow, he knew that he just didn't have it in him to thwart the command she'd given.

The low twang of metal hitting metal sounded from inside the forge, and he groaned. Damn the stubbornness of the woman.

He headed down the path towards the road. He'd left the others at the inn; if he joined them, they could regroup, talk strategy, work out what to do. Work out how in hell he was going to be able to persuade her to destroy her work.

He stopped dead to rights in the middle of the road. This wasn't just about Kenna destroying her work though; Nodens had insisted that she had to be stopped. Morcant knew from experience that the Godstouched were hard to stop. And she would be even more so. Nodens would want her, want that strength, extinguished. A car came around the bend and honked loudly, the driver gesturing furiously as he waved them on past him.

He'd known any number of Godstouched over the centuries, watched their power flare and then dissipate into nothingness when faced with a world where magic was almost extinguished; where it had been drawn back behind the Veil. There was just enough spark in certain places for it to be revived for a moment, perhaps two, but no longer. But here?

There were thousands of years' worth of life and death on the South Downs. Life that predated even his people's history. Where there was an intense history of settlements, the memory of the landscape preserved...*something*. He looked across the swell of the hills, the hedgerows teeming with life lining each side of the road, and took a deep breath.

He could feel it. Morcant's pulse quickened with excitement as he took another breath, and then another. The air felt alive. It was one of the few things that had made the Hunt seem bearable, air that hummed with life and kept your veins flush with magic. He and Deuroc, and later Aerten, had felt it the most. Something just beyond their reach.

As a whole, their Gods had disappeared with the Roman conquest, only Nodens left to mock their misfortune, and there'd been a lethargy to their faith. But now he wondered whether the Gods truly had left. Clearly not all of them, if the revival of Belisama and her followers—or follower—was anything to go by.

He started up again, walking swiftly down the quiet road. This changed, well, everything.

THE ATMOSPHERE INSIDE THE GOLDEN MARTLET WAS JOVIAL, and Morcant found the Hunt sat at a table, quaffing ale and looking really rather merry. After Deuroc had located Kenna's forge earlier, they'd left him to Nodens's quest and had clearly decided to take full advantage of having appetites once more.

Their table was strewn with empty plates and baskets filled with things in various shades of brown. Every now and then Sten slipped the Hound a morsel under the table, whilst the other three talked and laughed and drank.

He was momentarily struck by how eerily remnant it was of the last time they'd been able to feast, the feast in the Otherworld, but the moment passed the instant they all saw him.

"Morcant!" Herla stood and clapped him on the back, infused with the kind of energy he hadn't seen in his king in at least a millennium. "Tegan, a pint of Sussex Best for my friend here!"

The large woman behind the bar, a shock of silver-grey hair belying her youthfulness, raised a single eyebrow. "I've told you already, if you want serving, come to the bar. I'm not here to wait on you."

Herla chortled, which made her throw up her hands and

toss a dishcloth onto the bar. "You. Morcant. You want a drink? Don't just stand there, come on over."

He did as he was bid, Deuroc joining him as he ran his hands over the glossy maple of the bar, marvelling at the smoothness of its finish.

"I'll pay for his drink, Tegan."

She gave the blond man a look. "Sussex Best?"

"Yes." Deuroc's unwaveringly cheerful stare was unnerving enough even when you'd been used to it for centuries—he had the ability to almost see into your soul and do it without ever dropping his sunny grin—but this woman seemed completely unfazed by the Sage.

A snort and a "You want to stop staring and pay up?" accompanied two glasses of ale, but that was all.

When they made their way back to the rest of the Hunt, pints in hand, he looked at Deuroc. "How did you barter for money?"

"It was in the clothing that Nodens left for us."

Morcant slipped his hands into the built-in pouches within the legs and found coins of his own. "I see he thought of everything." His words were dry, bitter, and he realised that he very much resented the fact that they were having to lean on Nodens for anything.

"Better than dying of thirst. And we have food as well. But —" Concern flited across the other man's face.

"Yes?"

"What happened with the Godstouched?"

"I—" Morcant stopped, uncertain what to say next. He found himself loath to talk about it, to talk about Kenna. When he'd been given the quest, it was easy to talk about the Godstouched, to lay out his plan and outline what he was going to do to ensure their freedom. But now?

It had been a long time since he'd felt that...*something* for a woman. That urge to do anything, everything, just to see her smile. When stuck on a horse, with only a handful of people for company, there'd never been much point to it. Of the two women who'd ridden with them, Aerten wasn't interested in menfolk and Brianne had been of the Hunt for so fleeting a moment, that he'd never even had time to think of her like that. Of the women he'd seen over the centuries, it was hard to foster any kind of true emotion for someone whose life would be over in a fraction of yours. It had indeed been lonely, but the companionship of the Hunt had sustained him. That bond of kinship, of shared suffering, made them closer than a family ever could be.

So to be here, feet firmly planted on earth, he'd have thought that nothing other than making sure that neither he, nor they, would ever be trapped in the suffocating prison behind the Veil again would matter.

But he felt an intense unease at the prospect of 'stopping' Kenna. Her life was fleeting, especially compared to the centuries that he'd traversed. Surely just a passing fancy, and yet…

The woman with fiery hair and a fiery temper to match the flames she worked with, who stepped up to him, who challenged him and frustrated him and, Gods, he wanted her. He wanted to worship at the altar that was Kenna, and he wanted nothing more than to keep her as far away from Nodens and the horror—the torment—of being Godstouched for as long as possible. Especially when he knew she wouldn't just stop working with the goddess because he'd asked her. When he knew the Hunt's freedom was probably dependent on the kind of solution that made him want to drink himself into a stupor.

"Was it not her?" Deuroc was speaking again as they approached the table. "Because there's a few other Godstouched, Tegan at the bar, for one; but the woman in that building was by far the strongest."

"It was her." Morcant's voice sounded gruff, even to him. "But I have ale, and I want a memory to supplant the last time we drank. I want to forget that Godsdamned wedding feast and the Godsdamned Wild Hunt and just enjoy this moment with the five of us. The Godstouched can wait a few hours."

5

⚒⚒⚒

KENNA was loving this new project. She'd found herself imbued with a drive that had even made her forget about her ruined lunch—a rare occurrence indeed—and instead, everything in her had been focused on her work.

That's not to say that she wasn't usually driven, but there was something incredibly satisfying about putting aside the usual thoughts and intricate designs that accompanied a sculpting project and just giving herself over to the forge. Letting each ray of light find its way out of the copper and onto her anvil.

The light caught the warmth of the copper, and she paused momentarily, remembering the sheepish warmth of Morcant's smile before he'd gone all 'you can't do that' on her. Big and stubborn and…something intangible that made her roll her eyes. She wandered over to the door of the forge and peeked out. No sign of him.

She wasn't sure why that made her feel a little disappointed.

But the call of her work was too strong to resist, and Kenna went back to her anvil, running her hand over the most recently quenched piece. The curves she'd hammered into being and then polished into light-catching mirrors still felt warm beneath her touch, as if they truly were rays of light. There was a part of her that knew any kind of sense and logic had flown out of her mind following through on Belisama's request. But with each new piece she forged, with each piece that became more and more complete under her hammer, something akin to peacefulness overcame her.

Almost like some kind of meditation.

She'd always been a little bit sceptical of those lecturers at uni who'd argued art was experience. For her, forging was about function and place and less about the whole let's-stand-around-and-truly-appreciate-this-piece-of-art-you've-created-with-your-bare-hands thing. Especially as only a fool would forge without gloves. But now she kind of got it. She was part of the piece. Part of the art. Though she supposed it was hard not to be, when the flames you were using originated from your mouth.

Sweat trickled down the side of her face, and she brushed it roughly away with the back of her gloved hand and decided that it was unfair. Surely if she were the one wielding the flames, she should be impervious to their heat? But no, though her mouth was left unscorched, her hair was not impressed. Even with it shoved, unruly, into a topknot, she could feel the heat curling it into the kind of mess that rivalled what it looked like after a full day shoeing horses. That was going to be a fucker to untangle later.

A noise behind her from the office had her spinning round, hammer in hand. If Morcant was back, she'd physically toss him out of the forge. Damn well suplex him out the freaking door.

But the person in her office couldn't have been further from the man who'd occupied her thoughts for much of the afternoon. Arlee sat in Kenna's office chair, legs out of sight but clearly atop her desk, impishly grinning at her. "Hey."

"Hey." She leaned her hammer against the anvil and grinned at her friend. "I thought they didn't let teachers out during the day."

"Are you kidding?" Arlee swung their legs down and practically skipped across the forge. "Kenna, it's gone seven. I tried calling to see if you wanted to order a takeaway but to no avail. Clearly someone isn't hungry."

"Someone is most definitely hungry." She yanked the gloves off and tossed them onto the forge. "Managed to ruin my lunch, so I'm fairly ravenous." As she spoke, she realised exactly how hungry she was. If it had been an ordinary day forging using the furnace, she'd have been hungry enough, but all the fire breathing must have used more energy than usual. "Make that starving."

Her friend raised an eyebrow. "Pizza it is then. We should grab Rina, save her from what late-night hoodlums haunt the stacks of Tunford's library. I swear, the two of you never seem to stop working."

"Says you!" Kenna laughed, moving her tools to their place on her workbench. As much as Arlee teased both her and Rina into relaxing and taking a break, they'd never quite mastered the art of switching off themself, corralling swarms of ten-year-olds by day and piles of marking at night. Perhaps swarms was overstating it a little—Kenna had it on good authority that there were only twenty-four Year 6 children in Tunford Primary School—but on the few occasions when Arlee had brought the class down to the forge for a day trip in their role as Mx Richards, Kenna had been thoroughly overwhelmed. She had only just managed to stop herself threatening a particularly annoying wildling child with her trusty hammer.

"Right."

She paused for a moment, registering the dull note in her friend's voice, and she looked to where they stood, face carefully blank. "You okay, hun?"

"Tough day." They didn't say anymore, but they didn't need to.

"Definitely more than one pizza then." The three of them —her, Arlee, and Rina—had the same response to a really tough day: food, and lots of it. If it had been a Friday, they'd have been headed straight to the Golden Martlet and would probably have ended the evening begging Tegan to let them have a lock in—no matter that she'd never relented yet. But tonight was Thursday, a work night. A school night. And after a particularly messy Tuesday way back when, Arlee had put a kibosh on midweek drunken nights out because "Nothing makes a hangover more unbearable than squeaky ten-year-olds with no understanding of volume control." So, a takeaway had become their consolation for a terrible day, usually accompanied by some kind of beer and eaten cross-legged on the floor like they were students again.

Kenna went to grab her bag from the office and stopped, the melted and misshapen Tupperware box that had held her lunch catching her attention. How Arlee had managed to make her forget all about her morning—about the flames and the Goddess and Morcant's dark earnest eyes—she didn't quite know, but she was going to have to be super careful outside of the forge. As a blacksmith, she was more cautious than most about open flames—everyone knew that rolling hills and fields of crops didn't mix well with a lit match—but Goddess only knew what havoc fiery hiccups would cause. Kenna took a deep breath. Pizza. Pizza would make everything alright.

. . .

PIZZA HAD DEFINITELY BEEN A GOOD IDEA.

Kenna leaned against the sofa and said so. Loudly.

"Pizza's *always* a good idea," said Rina emphatically, "and not just because of its Italian origins." The woman had insisted on hosting tonight's takeaway feast, possibly because she had a coffee table the perfect height for mooching-on-the-floor eating, though she'd veritably forced coasters onto Arlee and Kenna when the beers had come out. Also, there was the whole fiercely-feeding-her-friends thing, which they all knew came down to the fact that when she couldn't fix things with books, Rina went all Italian on them and attempted to fix everything with food instead.

Arlee nodded vigorously and gestured wildly with their next piece of pizza. Kenna tried not to laugh as Rina's gaze anxiously followed the cheese dangling off the rogue slice. "Parents. Always thinking their *little darlings* are just *misunderstood.* Misunderstood my arse. That child is a menace!" The last word was punctured with a jab that made Kenna splutter with laughter, and then just as hurriedly, stop and cover her mouth in case of stray sparks.

Rina and Arlee swapped glances.

"What's going on?" asked Arlee.

"Huh?" She feigned innocence, which would have been easier to do if it had just been Arlee, the monarch of the tangential conversational route. Rina, however, was far harder to dissuade from her course.

"Something's clearly going on, Kenna," Rina said. "That's the third time this evening that you've covered your mouth like that."

"Don't get us wrong," Arlee interjected, "We're more than happy to be spared any infectious coughs or colds you might be harbouring, but you're not ill. Even I can tell that."

If it had been anyone else, Kenna would have made excuses. Hell, if it had even been her father—and she'd told him everything when he was still alive—she'd have made up something. Perhaps invented a chipped tooth or a cold that she didn't want to pass on. But these peeps were hers. They'd seen her through her father's death; they'd all turned up at Rina's part-time uni job after a sleezy bar manager had tried to feel her up and then pass it off as just banter; and they'd researched every queer- and nonbinary-friendly primary school in the whole of the South East until Arlee'd found a job where they were accepted. They'd lived together. They'd laughed and cried and ranted. They were hers, and they deserved more than lies and excuses.

"It sounds batshit," Kenna said.

They said nothing, no judgement, just waiting for her to continue.

"Fine." She got to her feet and strode across to where the living room met the kitchen, then turned when she realised they hadn't followed her. "You guys coming?"

"Oh, we're following, are we?" A lounging Arlee begged Rina for a hand up, and the two of them followed her curiously into the adjoining kitchen.

Rina's kitchen was immaculate. Clean, tidy, and everything in its place. Kenna couldn't help but wonder what it would look like all charred, a shell of its former self, as she turned the tap on, filling up the washing-up bowl in the sink basin with water. She turned to Rina. "Can you hold that?"

"I can hold it!" Arlee cut in.

"No, no," Rina said, "I'll need a mop if you're holding it; I've got it."

Kenna nodded and then grabbed some kitchen roll. The stand spun, and she accidentally tore more than the one piece she'd intended. "Fuck."

"Are you okay?" Even Arlee sounded sober this time.

"Yeah, I mean. Look, I just—" She cut off, unsure what to

say. At least with Morcant she hadn't had to say anything, he'd just *known*. But then again, he'd seen it.

She took a beat and then slowly, oh so carefully, she breathed a flame onto the paper in her hand. It danced silently across the white expanse, curling the paper in its wake, before she dropped it in the bowl Rina was holding. It extinguished with a long hiss.

Nothing.

She looked up. Cautiously. Rina's brow was furrowed, and Arlee's mouth was wide open. She'd actually managed to silence the teacher for the first time since she'd known them.

"Is it some kind of trick?" Rina's words were slow. Measured.

"No."

"So, you can just...breathe fire?"

The words hung there between the three of them, before Arlee grabbed another piece of kitchen roll and shoved it under Kenna's nose. "Do it again; I want to watch properly this time."

She did it again. And again. And would have done it a fourth time if Rina hadn't grabbed the roll from Arlee and muttered something about "Why didn't people waste their own paper towels instead of burning up the only kitchen roll in her flat."

Nothing. She didn't even dare raise her eyes to meet theirs. She'd expected some kind of response at least; incredulity, fear, anything but silence. "Well?"

"'Well?' You're asking *us*, 'Well?'!" Arlee's outburst left more than a little relief in its wake, and an eyeroll from Rina. "What the hell happened to you?"

Telling her best friends about accidentally summoning a goddess, being named her priestess, and being blessed with the ability to breathe fire wasn't something that Kenna would like to repeat, she decided afterwards. Arlee was way too excited about the whole thing and kept asking if she could do ridiculously dangerous things that hadn't even crossed Kenna's mind to attempt. Rina kept on talking about inner body temperatures and the importance of seeing a doctor. Right. Because what she needed was to explain that she could breathe fire to someone who'd either immediately palm her off on specialists who'd want to do an infinite number of tests on her or try to persuade her to sell her story to Channel Five for a *The Girl Who Breathed Fire* documentary. All she wanted to do was to keep forging. To work on her new project. To keep this to herself.

"You have to promise that you won't tell anyone." She sounded desperate, even to herself, and she clenched suddenly clammy palms. This couldn't get out. She needed it to remain a secret, because she didn't know what she'd do if people came barging in, trying to interrupt her work like Morcant had.

Kenna paused. She'd explained the goddess, the fire, all of that but… No. She didn't want to mention Morcant. Besides, he'd left her alone after she asked him to leave, and he hadn't actually done anything *wrong*.

And fine, maybe she didn't want to face the interrogation she knew would ensue. Her dark-haired stranger embodied her longing for that heady delight that came with power exchange, and that was something she wanted to keep to herself for now.

Or perhaps it was for a far more mundane reason: her friends' overexuberance. Because Rina seemed so excited about doing some research in the library the following day, and Arlee seemed so utterly delighted Kenna had actually opened up to them, for once, and shared something.

But if she was truly honest with herself, it was the way his gaze had dropped to her lips. As if he couldn't look away from them. From her. Yes, she had questions, and yes, she knew she should probably ask him for some more information about this whole Godstouched thing, but for now she kind of wanted to keep him to herself for just a little bit longer.

🔥🔥🔥

SO, IT WOULD APPEAR SPENDING THE EVENING QUAFFING ALE after two millennia of absolutely no quaffing whatsoever, was possibly not the best of ideas.

All five of the Hunt had eaten and drunk to their hearts' content, and though this was a far cry from the banquets of their past, it had seemed like nectar from the Gods. And clearly just as potent. The tavern itself had pretty much emptied, and its curvaceous landlady was now approaching them with a glint in her eye.

"Right, you guys. Night's over. Closing time."

Morcant followed Tegan's exasperated look and squinted in the direction of his companions. Herla was being held up by Sten and Aerten, both of whom seemed remarkably sober considering how much they'd drunk, and Deuroc had jumped to his feet as Tegan had walked over and was now swaying precariously.

The woman looked at the time piece on her arm and veritably growled under her breath. "I seriously don't have time for this. I need to close. Now."

Aerten spoke then, her calm demeanour never faltering. "This is a little unorthodox, but if we could rent some rooms, we'd be most grateful. And you'd be well compensated for your trouble."

Tegan sighed again and glowered at Herla when he opened his mouth to speak. "Mate, you'd be far better off letting your friend speak for you, because if I hear the word *wench* one more time, you'll be out on your ear. Aerten, is it? You seem sensible. I have"—she paused momentarily, before continuing on—"a family thing that I need to deal with, but I have two rooms available upstairs. Four beds. But you'll pay upfront, because I don't usually rent them out to strangers, and your dog can sleep down here by the fire."

Aerten and Sten exchanged glances and nodded.

"That'll do us nicely. Many thanks," said Aerten

"One of you'll have to kip on the floor, or something, that a problem?" she asked.

Morcant found himself speaking up, words appearing from somewhere and fighting to get off his tongue in a manner he vaguely recollected from his youth. "I don't need a bed, but thank you."

Tegan opened her mouth to ask, but closed it, clearly in a hurry. "Fine, whatever."

He waved away Deuroc's questions, and Aerten and Sten had been too focused on getting a near catatonic Herla up the stairs to pay him much attention. That was how Morcant found himself wandering along the road that led back to the forge but a few minutes later.

Twilight had always been his favourite time, even before the Hunt. There was something about the way silence seemed to truly have an almost tangible presence against a backdrop of the deepest blue. It reminded him of the stillest moments of the Hunt, of when they would look across sleeping hills and towns and not feel as though the world was rushing past them, leaving them behind.

He'd felt that stillness earlier that day when Kenna had met his gaze and the world had frozen. Stillness was precious. As he walked the path up to the forge itself, he thought of the Godstouched woman, with the fire in her eyes, breathing life back into that stillness.

There might be a way to circumvent Nodens's plans;

maybe. And whilst that was even a possibility, he'd protect her from anyone else who might come after her.

He clutched at the utensil in his hand, readying himself for anyone who might head towards the forge, towards Kenna, and leant back against the door to the forge, in a drunken watch.

6

⚒⚒⚒

"WHAT the fuck?"

Kenna looked at the sleeping figure leaning against the doorframe. She'd slept well once she'd gone to bed in her apartment above the forge, the exertion of playing with flames clearly having wiped her out. But she'd risen with the sunrise, finding herself itching to be downstairs. She'd usually be bleary-eyed and dying for coffee, but instead she was wide awake. What had Belisama said yesterday? *Goddess of Forge and Flame, of Crafts and Light.* She supposed the sun was made of flame, and it was certainly bloody light out here, so perhaps she'd be able to cut back on caffeine and make use of this whole priestess gig. And the first thing she'd do, was move this lump of a man out her doorway.

She nudged him gently with her shoe and moved back, bemused, as he jumped to his feet, waving around what appeared to be a fork.

"What've you got there, Morcant?"

He squinted at her and then, after his gaze finally focused, slumped back against the door. "Do you have to speak quite so loudly?"

Kenna leaned forward and plucked the fork from his grasp. "You are aware that this is a fork. And even if it were a knife, I'm fairly certain I could melt it on the spot. I could smelt it. With my fire-breath."

He shook his head and then cringed. "Not for you, for him. Gods it's bright out here."

She knew she should probably send him on his way, but she'd nursed a hungover Arlee too many times in their uni days to not recognise the signs of a particularly brutal hangover. And besides, if he'd actually been sat here all night, brandishing a fork in some misguided attempt to protect her forge, then she wanted to know what was going on. And possibly torture him a little by doing some forging.

She offered him a hand that he stared blearily at.

"Huh?"

"Look, you can either sit out here in the sun—which is only going to get brighter by the way—and flourish your fork at passers-by, or you can come inside, sleep your hangover off in my office, and then tell me what you're doing back here after I clearly sent you on your way yesterday."

There was a pause whilst he furrowed his brow and tried to make sense of his options, before cautiously taking her hand and allowing her to pull him up. He staggered slightly, and she grabbed the front of his shirt with her free hand, steadying him. He leaned into her, and she took his weight easily.

Damn. Even hungover the man was fine. And there was something about seeing a man like Morcant—someone who tossed out orders as if he were used to being obeyed—in a state like this. It showed an acceptance of vulnerability she didn't remember any of her exes showing her. There was something about him being this soft and slightly worn down in front of her, that made her want to soften towards him. Want to let him lean on her for a little longer. Want to feel more than just the callouses of his hand and the front of his shirt.

She dropped her gaze to where their hands still touched. She should let go. Let him go. But for some reason there was a comfort in him that belied his hungover state and made her feel warm, giving her fuzzy feelings that came with moments of caretaking. Though, to be fair, she wasn't entirely certain if he was hungover or if he was just still drunk.

"Are you okay?"

Kenna let go of his hand instantly, ignoring his questioning gaze, and walked through the door with a little more vigour than was entirely necessary, stifling a chuckle when he closed his eyes in what was clearly a hangover wince. "It's all good. Now go sleep off the booze and let me work."

As he stumbled towards her office, she took a deep breath. Thank Goddess for this project. She was going to need something to keep her mind off those eyes that searched hers for goodness only knew what. And off the way his clothed chest had felt beneath her hand.

Yeah, she was pretty certain that only the vibrating hum of hammered metal was going to be able to distract her from the fact that Morcant was curled up asleep in her office chair, and that she wanted to go in and check on him.

MORCANT HAD BEEN FAIRLY CERTAIN THERE WAS NO WAY HE was going to be able to sleep through the clanging and banging of the forge, especially when each thud of the hammer resulted in sparks that made his head throb. But all that ale the night before had had a bigger impact on him than he'd realized. He was alarmed when Kenna woke him, clearly some hours later, by shoving a bowl of broth under his nose.

"That should help bring you back to the land of the living."

He nodded and took it from her, glad the world was no longer dancing a jig that would send him stumbling across the room. One spoonful and he was overcome with hunger, barely stopping to thank her as he scoffed down the entire bowl. When he finished, he looked up to see her eyeing him curiously. "Thank you?"

"You're welcome." She took the dish from him and placed it on the side. "This is a one-off thing though; don't expect to be fed every time you turn up here like a lost puppy. Now, what on earth were you doing? Because if you're here to tell me what I can and can't make again…?"

"No. I'm not." Her gaze met his and once more he was struck by the depth within them. There was something so vibrant about her, as if she were the embodiment of life itself, a whirlwind of action caught up in one human body. A vibrancy that was threatened by his very freedom, by the recklessness of the Gods. "I think you're in danger."

"From Belisama, yeah, you said." She ran a hand through her hair in exasperation. "Is there anything I can say that'll persuade you that a) I'm a big girl, I can look after myself, and b) she's the last person I need protecting from?"

"You're…very strong. And independent."

"Of course!" She sounded indignant that he'd ever doubted this would be the case. In fact, Morcant couldn't imagine this fireball of a woman being anything but strong. It was imbued in every line of her body, from the way she held herself, to her confidence. It was even in the way she met his eyes; challenging and completely unafraid. "I make my own decisions, and you don't get to make those for me."

This was going wrong. Fast. He needed to say something,

anything, that showed he was listening. That he did believe her. "No, of course."

"And I really don't need protecting by a drunk guy with a fork. What on earth did you think you'd be able to accomplish with that?"

He felt himself flush. That was more than a little embarrassing. "Like I said to you yesterday, I've been trapped as a member of the Wild Hunt for millennia. There wasn't much opportunity for...ale."

"Ah." Kenna's eyes twinkled, and he got the distinct impression she was rather amused by the whole thing. "No alcohol tolerance?"

"I can drink! Or, I could, but it appears these days my fortitude may be a little...lacking."

She muttered something under her breath that sounded suspiciously like she didn't think he was lacking in many other departments, as she wiped her hand across her forehead. Morcant felt his heart swell. And other parts of him. He looked around desperately, in an attempt to find something to distract his attention away from the sweat streaking down the curve of her neck. He wanted to dip his head to taste it, to kiss her there until she gasped with pleasure and—no. *No.* There was something in him, some longing that had been caged over the centuries, that was awakening with every look they exchanged. In fact, it may well have awakened that moment when she'd touched her hammer to his shoulder.

"I... I... Can I look at your work?" he asked.

This time, her gaze softened. "You want to see my work?"

"Yes." The moment he answered her, he knew it was true. He could tell, just from being in this little room off the forge, how much power was emanating from it. He was longing to see what it was she was pouring so much of herself into, to see what it was that had her working herself into a sweat. Her work was clearly important to her, a form of self-expression, and he wanted to see more. Art was supposed to be an insight into the soul of the artist, right? And he knew there was no one else who he wanted more insight into. "Please?"

She nodded slowly, and he followed her across to where some metal lay on a workbench. One piece of copper, perfectly polished, caught the light as if it were a shaft of light itself. "Wow. It looks so…"

He touched the shining piece tentatively and felt a flash of something sharp and hot judder up his arm before he fell into darkness.

7

⚒⚒⚒

OKAY, so this was now getting more than a little ridiculous. First, she had to contend with Goddesses appearing up out of nowhere, then she started breathing flames, and now one of her pieces had given Morcant what had looked like an acute electric shock, and now he was passed out on the floor.

Enough was enough.

It had all been fine and dandy, but now someone had got hurt. And not just someone, the only person she'd met who seemed to have the slightest idea of what was going on. Morcant was sweet, and kind of adorable when he got that dazed look in his eyes. He'd backed off when she told him to, had attempted to drunkenly protect her forge with a fork—which was more amusing than she'd given him credit for—and he seemed to actually listen to her. She liked that. She liked that he'd done as he was told and got some sleep and had eaten his chicken soup without complaint. And she liked that he'd been interested in her art and *fuck this.*

She didn't like that this had resulted in him getting hurt.

She wasn't supposed to let him get hurt.

As she moved him into the recovery position, his shirt rode up, revealing a very nice set of abs. Kenna jerked her hands back. She was very firmly *not* ogling the gorgeous man. It was fine. He was breathing, and she'd done the right thing, health and safety wise. If he didn't wake up within an hour, she'd call an ambulance—though how she'd explain to the paramedics that it was her magic, fire-breath-forged metal that made him pass out, she didn't know. Swiftly, she went to the workbench to tidy the metal pieces.

Her hands shook as she placed the copper back how it had been, and she stretched her fingers out, not wanting to keep touching the metal and yet…she *needed* to.

She tentatively picked up the piece Morcant had touched and watched the light dance across its surface. Nothing happened. So, what the hell had happened to him? This was the only piece she'd polished on the grinder until it was so smooth you could see your reflection in it; at least, the only piece so far. She'd started on it first thing that morning, whilst Morcant had been snoring in her office, hoping to get a polish on a couple of them before moving on to the next pieces that needed forging. But after that one piece, the need to get back to the physicality of hammer on metal had been too strong. She'd been drawn to the anvil, drawn to directing her art, her heat, her flames into this piece.

Shuddering, she let it drop.

That need was strong now, even with Morcant on the floor. and yet she couldn't stop herself from reaching out again and running her index finger along the curved edge of the metal, marvelling at what she'd made.

This. This was why she forged. The heat, the sparks, the hiss of the metal when you quenched it, all of that faded into insignificance when she considered the fact that she made this. Her. Not a machine, not someone else with years of experience, but her. And the transformation from dull metal to shiny ray of light? That metamorphosis was more precious than she knew how to put in words. Every time she walked past one of her pieces in the village, from the railings round the pond to the iron that held the Golden Martlet's sign, she knew she was at home. That connection between her art and her community made her feel like she fit here. Like each piece was a bit of her; forever part of the landscape, forever belonging to this place.

"So this is what the Godstouched are doing these days."

There was something in the unknown man's voice that made her reach out for her hammer before facing the surprise visitor behind her. One glance at the door showed it still closed, and yet here he was, standing in her forge, looking around as though he owned the place. Tall, dark, with features that seemed to shift as shadows fell across his face.

Something brushed against her mind, and she felt sparks as her own new power put up a resistance. Taking a step back, she levelled her hammer in his direction. "Tell me who you are." No questions. No weakness. Kenna didn't quite know how, but she knew, surer than anything she'd ever known, that even the slightest bending of her will would have catastrophic events.

"She must be having such fun with you. Fool should have stuck with the Ancients like I did; they're far less inclined to shows of impudence."

Her eyes moved involuntarily to where Morcant lay on the floor, and he, it, laughed. *"Morcant the Ancient. Indeed. Impressive though, laying him out like that. You're clearly more powerful than I expected; I don't suppose you'd care to switch sides? Channel some of that power into something a little more daring, rather than letting it burn you up?"*

Strengthening her resolved, she took a small step forward. "This is my forge. My place of power. And you have no right to be here. Leave." Short. Sharp. Concise. Everything that she did when she was most nervous. Some people babbled—Arlee was a babbler—but when Kenna was frightened, only her thoughts ran wild. "And I don't switch sides. I'm the Smith. A priestess of the forge and the fire. Take it up with Belisama."

As she spoke, heat flared from the corner of the forge where her commission stood. Clearly Belisama had heard her name and had decided to pay her another visit.

Kenna wasn't sure whether she was pleased for the backup, or frustrated with the need for it. Whoever he was, this god—for he was most definitely a god—made her feel very uneasy indeed. Far too smarmy for her liking. And when Belisama finally spoke, it was clear she wasn't overly fond of the interloper either.

"You!" The single word was filled with such anger that she winced away from the blast of heat that accompanied it. The goddess had wrapped herself once more in Kenna's forged flames, but they were an icy blue as opposed to the warmth of the golden flames she'd seen on the goddess's first appearance. Blue flames were hotter, and Belisama's temper was clearly flaming along with her robes. *"You dare to enter my priestess's temple?"*

Temple. Huh. Kenna found herself wondering whether she should perhaps put that above the door. *Blacksmith's Forge and Temple. Visit for Damascene metalwork, architectural structures, and incense.* It certainly had a ring to it, tripped off the tongue even. Perhaps she should think about having it made. She looked around and wondered whether either of them would notice if she just backed out and left them to it.

The contrast between the two gods was eerie. Belisama all flaming anger and the other all shifting shadows. She blinked and tried to focus on him but found her eyes skating over his face, unable to fix on any particular feature. Creepy. Even his voice seemed shifty, smooth and silky, like he was trying to seduce the goddess into silence.

Belisama, however, was bellowing at him. *"This is my space; my sacred space. You dare come here and try to steal my priestess? Take the cursed one and leave."*

"If I could just interrupt you for a minute."

Kenna had the very uncomfortable experience of having two gods looking directly at her, and neither seemed overly delighted at being interrupted.

"What?" bit out the shadowy god, before the goddess turned on him furiously.

"You dare speak to my priestess like—"

"Yes, yes," interjected Kenna hurriedly. "He's an arse who thinks he can talk to women however he likes. We've all met them. But about the cursed thing…"

"We have indeed all met them." She could have sworn the goddess's flames softened slightly, a trace of warmth creeping into their flickering light. *"What about the 'cursed thing'?"*

"Morcant's cursed? Because he touched one of my pieces? That doesn't seem all that fair, and if I'm being completely honest your Goddessness, I don't think I'm going to be letting *him*"—she gestured towards the shadowy god with her head—"take anyone anywhere." She moved in what she assumed would appear like a foolish act of defiance, and which certainly felt like one, in between the gods and the prostrate Morcant. Morcant who, despite all the commotion, still hadn't come around.

She could have sworn something akin to a smile flickered across Belisama's face, and her shoulders unclenched, her hands loosening themselves from the fists that they'd formed.

But a cold, sharp laugh emanated from the other shadowy god. *"You think that you can stop me from taking him?"*

The room visibly darkened, and she felt herself shrink

away from where the shadows surrounding him grew. They scuttled across the floor, almost alive, and she swung her hammer at them. Each time she caught one with the tip of her hammer, it struck something solid, and sent them flying back away from her.

"You think that you, or your precious goddess can possibly stop me? I, who have had millennia of worship and tribute laid at my feet? You think your fading flames can stand in my way?"

The shadows came faster and faster, and she saw one fly up the goddess's robe, dousing one of the flames. Belisama met her eyes and with an apologetic look, fled the statue, leaving it lifeless in her wake.

"Shit."

Her muttered curse seemed to summon even more of the shadows, all scuttling towards her, attempting to dodge the arc of her hammer as it swung around.

"You think that puny manmade thing can stand up to my shadows? Well, you are nothing if not spirited."

His words stoked a furnace within her. Spirited? Fuck spirited. She was the Smith. This was *her* forge, and she'd be damned if anyone tried making demands of her in here. She opened her mouth to retort and instead roared at him. Admittedly, there were definitely flames on her breath, so she was kind of purposefully breathing fire in his direction, but she was more than a little taken aback by the whole roaring thing. Almost as if from afar, she heard herself roar again. And again. And then, as the last roar burst aflame from her throat, something snapped inside her.

She was vaguely aware of the shadows fading away, of the god's presence lessening until it no longer took up space in her forge, but at the forefront of her mind was the pain. She fell to all fours and roared again, though this time it had very little to do with anger. This pain, this unbearable searing that etched itself on each and every limb. It felt as though her arms and legs were being stretched beyond recognition, and her back? It felt like it was being ripped apart.

She straightened her arms out in front of her—anything to try and lessen the agony—and tried desperately to latch onto something with the claws she saw before her. Rearing up, Kenna found the floor falling away, further and further until her head knocked on the high beams of the forge's roof. Turning this way and that, spinning round, all she caught was glimpses of deep red, of flames dancing along the edge of the copper rays on her workbench, and then, at last, she caught a glimpse of herself in the polished mirror of the ray that had shocked Morcant into unconsciousness.

She was a fucking dragon.

CHAPTER 8

INTERLUDE

RINA Baroni was the kind of librarian who, when faced with the kind of situation that puzzled her, turned to what she understood best. Books. Friday afternoons were always quiet in the library, the local aging population off galivanting in the church hall for their weekly luncheon, so she'd managed to persuade Lenna Harris, head librarian, that the 'Local Information' shelving could do with some tidying up and reshelving. English villagers had a fascination with their own backyard she was only truly appreciating right this moment.

Her goal? To find information about anything that was known for breathing fire within the South Downs area. Rina had taken a few 'toilet breaks' more than usual, to check out Belisama during the day. The goddess seemed to be a bit of an enigma, a quick Wikipedia search turning up some information about her worship in France, and a river in Lancashire that might have been named after her in Roman times, but nothing of any actual use for Kenna. But fire-breathing entities in Sussex and on the South Downs? That she could do.

For one thing, there was a veritable smorgasbord of books on Sussex and the South Downs in this clearly very popular section of the library, and as she started reorganising the books available (for what kind of librarian would allow shelves to sit in such an unordered state? Mr. Melvil Dewey would have been horrified), she used footnotes and references to find her way through to the kind of myths and legends Kenna might find helpful.

She wasn't naïve enough to think Kenna would actually go to a doctor for the whole fire-breathing thing. She and Arlee had had to drag the redhead to the GP when she'd got a chest infection in their second year at uni, and Kenna'd only allowed it because she'd coughed at a vital point in the soldering part of her art project and ruined some delicate work she'd been slaving over for weeks. Her friend was stubborn as hell and seemed to equate something as basic as going to the doctor with taking up space she shouldn't. Rina personally thought it had something to do with how Kenna had been brought up by her father after her mother had left, but any kind of discussion following that line of thought was dismissed with a raised eyebrow and a very determined change of subject. Indeed, if left to her own devices, Kenna would probably just muddle along, fire-breathing in her own way, with a distinct lack of interest in anything even slightly similar to her own situation. And the only legends Rina could think of that yelled fire-breathing were dragons.

There were a few dragon-related myths from Sussex she could find. One outside Lyminster where a water dragon was supposedly killed by a wandering knight, who got offered up an unsuspecting and probably unwilling princess as a reward, and another dragon St Leonard had apparently killed out near Horsham. Rina thought it rather unfair the dragons, these strong and powerful creatures, were always stamped out by humans She was about to abandon dragons in the hope of finding something a little more concrete, when her eye fell upon a reference to the Dragon of Bignor Hill. One sentence jumped out at her with such clarity she almost dropped the book.

One such, of whom little is remembered, is said to have lived on Bignor Hill, where the marks of his coils were still to be seen winding round the hillside.

She went to close the book and put it back on the shelf and then stopped. There was something niggling in her mind, just out of touch, and she found herself reaching for an Ordinance Survey map. Checking round the corner of the shelf for Lenna, she spread the map out on the table closest to her. As her eyes fell upon the words Bignor Hill, she felt a tremor. Grabbing the table, she watched as the map unfurled, each contour line rising out of the paper until she was looking at what seemed like a three-dimensional video feed of Bignor Hill itself.

What the actual...?

Fighting the urge to grab a pen and paper to make notes, Rina took in the image of a dragon, coiling itself around the hill before taking off, leaving chalky paths in its wake. The flying figure moved across the map, contours rising and falling as it passed, until it landed in a wooded area, and the image folded back into the map, leaving a cross on the spot where the dragon had landed.

Rina fell into a chair. Well, that certainly had given her

more information than expected. She could have questioned it, could have wondered about the hows and the wherefores, but doing so seemed counterproductive, especially when Kenna had proved the improbable last night. The best thing to do, she decided, was to claim back some of the flexitime her boss had promised her, and head over to the forge right this minute. Because if anyone could explain to Kenna the pros and cons of breathing fire, it'd be the dragon she somehow *knew* was alive and kicking in the South Downs.

IT WAS PROBABLY BECAUSE SHE'D SEEN A MAP COME TO LIFE IN her own sleepy library that morning, but Rina was surprisingly unsurprised by the sight of a red dragon flying out of Kenna's forge as she made her way up the road. The creature hovered for a few minutes in the air, flapping its wings in what was clearly a fuck-these-things-better-keep-me-aloft panic, before zooming upwards like a fizzy drink bottle in a science experiment. And Rina knew it was Kenna, just like she'd known the dragon in the map was real and alive. She couldn't have said how she knew; she just did.

Rather than questioning what seemed a certainty to her, she peered after the disappearing figure of her friend, *the dragon,* and turned a slowly hardening face towards the forge. Clearly something had startled Kenna, and Kenna did not startle easily.

But when she entered the forge, it seemed completely empty. Her friend's hammer was in the centre of the floor, not even leaning against the anvil. The pieces of copper—some dull, one glinting—abandoned on the workbench. And of course, the door left wide open. Rina had never seen it left like that. Kenna wasn't exactly the friendliest of smiths and discouraged strangers from coming in and interrupting her work.

Rina picked up the hammer to move it and, all at once saw a shadow of Kenna on all fours, wings ripping out of her misshapen back as she writhed in agony. She saw a shadowy man walking out on her friend's pain. And she saw a deathly still figure behind her transforming friend.

Blinking, her vision cleared, but there, on the floor in the corner, was that same still figure. She hurried over to the dark-haired man, then breathed a sigh of relief when she realised he was merely passed out, not dead. A dead man might have been one shock too far.

She grabbed a chair from Kenna's workbench and placed it on the floor by the unconscious man. She sat there for a couple of minutes before realizing that if she wanted answers when he awoke, sitting meekly like this wouldn't get them. Rina briefly contemplated grabbing the abandoned hammer but dismissed the idea. She wouldn't be able to get the balance right in her hand and was more likely to injure herself than anything else. Instead, she headed into Kenna's office to grab the librarian's greatest weapon: a book with some serious heft. She knew there was one in there somewhere, because Rina's congratulations-on-getting-your-own-forge present for her friend had been a book on blacksmithing. And sure enough, there it was. *Practical Blacksmithing* had over a thousand pages of illustrations and tables. Hefty. Heavy. A threat in the hands of an angry librarian. And, as she weighed the hardback tome in her hands, it definitely seemed to fit the current moment.

CHAPTER 9

MORCANT'S head spun as his vision slowly came back into focus. The silence in the forge made him wonder where Kenna had gone, before he looked up to see a dark-haired, stony-eyed, Roman-looking woman staring at him. She leaned over the back of the chair she straddled, shifting an alarmingly large book from one hand to the other threateningly.

"Um, hello?" The question sounded weak, even to his own ears, and she raised an eyebrow silently. Well, this was more than a little unnerving. He was used to Kenna's fiery temperament, but this woman seemed calm and collected, and possibly slightly angry? He wasn't sure, and with Deuroc's words about other Godstouched being in the vicinity, he wasn't about to annoy anyone else if he could help it. "Do you know where Kenna is? She was here mere moments ago…" He looked around the forge for any sign of the redhead, but she was nowhere to be seen.

"She flew out of here."

The curt sentence was cold, but he opened his mouth

nevertheless to ask in which direction she'd been headed before the woman added, "Literally." He shut it.

She stood up. "I think you have some explaining to do. I'd quite like to know how my best friend turned into a dragon, and what exactly you did to exacerbate the situation."

A dragon?

Morcant was stunned. Not at the prospect of dragons—the Hunt had seen echoes of their presence on multiple occasions over the years—but a Godstouched having the ability to shift into one? That hadn't happened since before the Roman occupation, when magic was at its height, and the gods were far more inclined to interfere in mortal lives. He supposed it made sense—the flames on her breath, the patronage of Belisama, her working with precious metal—but still. He looked at the woman in front of him, one hand on her hip, the other balancing the heavy book on her shoulder. "I didn't know she was a dragon shifter, but it makes sense. And as to my involvement, well I can tell you up until the moment when I passed out, Miss…?"

"Rina." She sat back down abruptly. "I'm Rina. Who are you?"

"I'm Morcant." He hesitated for a moment and then added, because the woman had seen a dragon without dissolving into complete hysterics, and because this probably was all his fault after all, "I'm a member of the Wild Hunt."

⁂

KENNA COULDN'T QUITE BELIEVE IT.

The rolling hills of the South Downs lay before her like a blanket, as if she were watching the video feed of a drone flying over the landscape instead of experiencing the glory of flight for herself. The moment she considered the actual situation, she wobbled a little. It was as though actually thinking about flying was enough to throw her off balance. The last thing she wanted was to come hurtling out of the sky and crash-land in a field filled with cows—she had experience with cows; she suspected they would be anything but understanding.

She raised her head carefully upwards and stretched out the elongated neck that was apparently now hers.

Up until this moment, Kenna realised she'd never truly appreciated the sky. It sounded foolish—certainly felt like a foolish thought to have—but there was something about the way in which it went on forever she found rather comforting. Whether human or dragon, she didn't take up much space. Not in the grand scheme of things. She was still just one being, muddling along. Or, she supposed, flying along.

When she'd first taken off, startled by the reflection of red scales and large amber eyes in the copper she'd abandoned on the anvil, she'd flapped frantically and then ended up just heading in one aimless direction. She was too nervous to turn or to try and control where she was going. At the back of her mind, there'd been a fair amount of self-satisfaction, especially when she considered the fact that not even a weird shadow god had wanted to take her on. Her forge could be a haven from interfering gods and goddesses who just couldn't help but butt in on perfectly normal and content people's lives.

But then, there'd been the realisation that the ability to protect people from the veritable pantheon of gods who seemed to be coming out of the shadows was pretty useless unless she managed to gain some control over where she flew.

She tried, tentatively, edging a wing upwards in a motion that changed her course. *Hmmm.*

She dropped it down, and her path straightened out.

She tried the other. The same thing happened.

Okay. So, she could navigate. And turn around if she needed. What next?

That was the biggest question. What the hell was going to happen next? Firstly, she needed to put controlling her shifting abilities (holy fuck, she had shifting abilities) at the top of the list. Changing in the forge hadn't been too bad, what with its high ceilings, but if she'd been in an enclosed space… She shuddered, and the little spark from her snout extinguished as it got caught on an air drift. Either she'd have exploded out, or… Neither prospect appealed.

She slowly circled round, careful to remain high enough so any shadow she cast onto the farmland below would merely look like a passing cloud. She knew she should go back. Should return to where she'd left a passed out Morcant and work out what next to do, but she didn't much like her chances if the shadow god came back. But then again, if she didn't go back, she didn't much like Morcant's chances either. At least she knew she could go all dragon on shadow god's arse and chase him out. Better than the alternative, at least.

Right. Forge-ward it was.

SHE CHOSE TO DESCEND AROUND THE BACK OF THE FORGE, away from where the road met the path to her workshop and where prying eyes might conceivably alight upon the… the creature she now was. Descend was a pretty word for what actually happened, which was more akin to desperately trying to slow down before crashing into a tree, being sent scrambling backwards on all fours until she landed with an actual audible thump on her arse.

It took her a moment to adjust to her new surroundings,

before she realised there were two humans looking at her, rather curiously.

"Kenna?"

That was Rina, her face pale with concern. Kenna huffed and gently nudged the woman's shoulder with her snout in an attempt to reassure her.

Morcant stood behind her friend, and when she lifted her gaze, it met his with a magnetism that felt like it should have some kind of sound accompanying it. Trumpets perhaps. Or maybe a cymbal clash. His mouth curled up in a slight smile, and she felt it all the way down to her toes, like a warmth spreading throughout whatever extremities dragons had. She sighed, and when she did, she physically felt the scales fall away. As if she were wearing a wetsuit that could be peeled back until she was standing there, her human eyes still meeting his, feeling that feeling in actual toes.

Rina squawked awkwardly, but it wasn't until her friend spun away, hurriedly saying something about a lack of clothes, that Kenna realised she was naked. And logically she knew she should cover up, to save Rina's blushes at least, but she couldn't help but stand there, flushed and revelling at Morcant's eyes widening and filling with the warmth of desire. His gaze, tight on hers, felt like a caress, as if he were standing mere inches from her and she could sense his longing, feel the electricity in the air between them. His jaw tightened, and he blushed. Dropping his eyes to the ground, he shucked off his jacket and thrust it in her direction.

She took the jacket and silently slipped it on, the oversized leather hitting her upper thighs. It covered her just about enough so she could let Rina know that it was okay to turn around again.

"Not that you aren't immensely attractive," her friend apologised once she was facing Kenna again, "but it's been far too long since I've seen a naked woman, and I'm a little weirded out by the fact that it's you."

Morcant said nothing. She shot a glance at him, and he was looking right at her. His eyes implied that he hadn't been weirded out at all, and that he'd like nothing better than for her to slip out of the jacket and make him kiss her into ecstasy, right here behind the forge. The jolt of awareness between them, the acknowledgement of their mutual attraction, had her breasts aching. She wanted him.

She swallowed and quickly looked away, trying to ignore the searing heat of desire that her skin was aflush with. "So, Rina. I don't suppose you know anything useful about dragons?"

Rina, it turned out, not only knew about dragons, but also something very useful about Sussex dragons and those residing on the South Downs. She supposed that she shouldn't be surprised her friend had hit the books. Rina had always loved a good research project, but all Kenna could think was she was supremely thankful for her friend's due diligence in researching whatever she could about fire-breathing. There was all the info she was able to give Kenna about dragons—that was unparalleled—but there was also the realisation that Kenna was not the only one who'd been affected by whatever the Gods appeared to have put into Tunford's water supply.

This discovery finally diverted Morcant's attention away from her as he listened to Rina's story of moving maps and visions.

"Another of the Godstouched. You did not mention these visions before."

Rina raised an eyebrow. "Mention the weird visions I've only just experienced to the millennia-old guy that used to be part of an otherworldly hunt and whose arrival timed itself with all the bizarre shit happening around here? No, it *didn't* seem like the best idea at the time."

Kenna snorted. The librarian usually skirted conflict with a quietly lethal calm, but she'd apparently decided that, for all her cutting words, Morcant wasn't a bad guy. The sarcasm characterised the Rina only a few ever got to know.

"And no," Rina continued, before he could talk, "No goddess for me. I'm just a plain old visionary."

"Oracle," he said, "That's usually the term given to those who can do what you can do."

Rina nodded slowly, clearly storing the information away for another research session, before refocusing on Kenna. "Oracle or not, you need to speak to someone who knows how to control… contain… whatever this is you're going through. And who better than another dragon?"

"Another dragon?" Kenna's heart thumped. Another dragon would mean someone who understood, who knew what it was, why it was, that she was like this. "Where?"

The librarian strode in the direction of the forge door. "I've a map in my bag." When no one immediately followed, she turned and shook her head. "You need the blow by blow? Fine. The maps… in the books… I mean…"

Kenna had never seen her friend stutter over words so. "Rina?"

The brunette took a deep breath and started again. "It's real, okay? Those winding sheep paths round Bignor Hill? Turns out they actually *were* made by dragon scales, and I can show you on a map where that dragon went. It was"—she flushed and raised her eyebrows at Kenna—"I imagine it was like you finding out that you can turn into a dragon. Throws you slightly off-kilter, and I'm sure I'll process it all at some point, but right now, you are what matters. So, let's get you to that dragon."

WHEN MORCANT HAD OFFERED UP A HORSE, THE TWO women had looked at him in complete confusion. It wasn't that bizarre; Kenna had needed to get across country, and he'd be able to get her there faster than any machine. Well, possibly not, but he wouldn't like to chance a car in an area so utterly drenched in magic as a dragon's lair.

"I can't ride a horse though." She'd ran a hand through those unruly red locks of hers, the colour spilling across her pale skin like fire over water.

"You could ride on the back of mine. I can ride, and you can navigate." His groin had tightened at the idea of her on his mount, arms clasped round him, breasts brushing against his back as they headed across the Downs, and he'd fought to regain control of himself.

She'd acquiesced, and so now he was waiting outside the forge for her to return. She'd gone to get clothes, he assumed, now that her earlier outfit was in tatters in a corner of the workshop. For a moment, he remembered her standing there, defiantly naked, her entire being throbbing with the kind of post-shift power that made him want to lose himself in her. Morcant tried to pretend that the irresistible draw to power was all it had been, a magical echo reverberating through him. But if that had truly been the case, he wouldn't have found himself hardening now at the remembrance of the knowing curve of her lips promising heat and desire and the ability to feel more alive than he'd ever been before.

He shook his head sharply, surprising the beautiful horse who'd been his mount for all of those deadening years. He blew down her nostrils, calming Steorra. Gently stroking her back until he felt his hand hit the supple leather of a saddle. He froze.

Dear Gods, he was actually going to do it. Remount.

It was at once both a blessing and a curse. The fact that he could do this and then get down was a freedom that he'd never thought to have again, but at the same time... What if it all went wrong? What if Nodens had a fit of pique and changed his mind somewhere along the way? Would he be stuck once more?

If he had to leave the world again it might kill him. He'd rather dismount into oblivion than continue in that half-life.

Morcant's hands bunched up in the reins, and he found himself close to breaking. Those years, all of those years of never interacting, never truly *living*. It was too much for any man to bear. And for all the comradeship he felt for the rest of the Hunt, for the men and women who'd lasted throughout as well as those who'd fallen behind, he wanted a chance to be something other than Nodens's mouthpiece as the bearer of bad tidings. The one whose words caused heartache and pain and—

He felt a hand, gentle on his shoulder, and he tensed before he heard her words. "Morcant? Are you alright?"

Was he alright? He was hit suddenly by a realization that he *had* felt alright, he'd felt, well...*normal*. There was something about the last few days that made all those years in limbo fade away. Reins fell from his grasp, and he slowly moved until he was facing her.

"Morcant?"

Kenna's head was tilted on one side, at once curious and concerned, and he wanted to kiss her more than anything. It wasn't just desire, though he'd be lying if he said he didn't want her, but also a longing to bring her joy and excitement. To make her feel alive the way she'd brought him back to life. To worship her.

"Kenna," he breathed out.

She must have seen something in his eyes, because her lips parted slightly, and with a smile he felt down in the very depths of his soul, she lifted her hand to cup his face. His hand mirrored hers, caressing her skin until his thumb fell to the soft swell of her lips. Her sharp inbreath galvanised him.

Then Kenna pulled, moulding her curves to his body as she took his mouth with hers.

CHAPTER 10

SHE was done with words. Everything about the last two days had been weighed down with words which tried to explain the inexplicable. Her transformation into a dragon, the discovery that her best friend was some kind of oracle. And him.

Screw explanations.

What she wanted—what she *needed*—right now was exactly this; to be in the moment, to live like she'd flown, completely and utterly present. So, when he raised his head and looked at her, his pupils dark and dilated, her name breathed out like a question, she'd bridged the gap between them. As their lips met her hand snaked up, entangling fingers in his short hair, the feel of him grounding the electricity that shot across her skin.

The next thing she knew, they were stumbling backwards until she felt the rough brick of the forge scratching against her jeans, and then their kiss became a blur of lips and hands and tongues. The skin at his neck was hot under her hands and she wondered whether he was as flushed as her. Because she certainly felt flushed; her entire body thrummed with heat and desire. She was lightheaded as they came up for air —almost drunk as she pulled him back, determined to satiate her thirst for him. His hands moved to her breasts, pausing before she arched towards his touch so they filled his hands. Even through the fabric of her shirt and the lace of her bra, her nipples tightened with desire, hardening against the shadow of his heated touch.

She wasn't sure she would ever have enough of his touch. She craved the feel of his hands, calloused from millennia of riding, against her skin. She wanted to banish the fabric between them, to touch him in the way he so clearly wanted to touch her, until they both were slick with desire and want. She released a shaky breath, and her hands trembled where they caressed the nape of his neck.

He lifted his mouth and rested his forehead against hers, his breath jagged and desperate. She took in a fractured breath of her own and huffed out a short laugh they both knew was more longing than amusement. "Morcant? You okay?"

When his eyes met hers this time, Kenna's knees went wobbly, and she was beyond grateful for the wall against her back. She'd never seen someone look at her with such intense longing before. As if he was drinking in the sight of her. As if she was all he needed to sustain himself.

"Okay does not even begin to describe how I feel right now." His voice was a husk that she felt down in her very core.

"Oh." Well, to be fair, that was a pretty good summation of how she felt. Her body thrummed with awareness of him that seemed to seep into her very muscles, and she couldn't really concentrate on anything other than the fact that she could feel him, hot and hard against her thigh. So damn close to where her need left her slick with desire.

"Kenna, you make me feel—" He cut off, as if he were

searching for words, any words, that could encapsulate the near physical spark of attraction between them. "You make me feel *everything*." That last word, dissipating into the air as if he were breathing his truth, caught at her. "I want this, more than anything, but the dragon..."

"The dragon?" For a moment, she wasn't sure what he was talking about. Did he mean her dragon? Did shifting change her ability to have sex? Fuck, she hoped not. That'd be really, really shit.

He laughed softly and kissed her so gently that she wanted nothing more than to push him to the floor and tell him to kiss her all over, just like that. "The Dragon of Bignor Hill. The one your friend Rina gave us directions towards. We should probably…"

"Oh *that* dragon!" Her cheeks heated. Damn libido, making her a momentary amnesiac. "I mean, we totally should, yeah."

One long lingering look that almost had her reaching for the button of her jeans and then he was stepping away, turning towards the horse that was still tethered to the post outside the forge. The animal seemed to be looking at them in what she was convinced was bemusement. Damn thing was clearly far too attached to her Morcant.

To Morcant. Not *her* Morcant. For fuck's sake.

Kenna was about to continue to mentally admonish herself for when she realised, he was taking the saddle off his horse.

"Wait a sec." She didn't love horses. Didn't really even like them. And she certainly didn't like where this was going.

"Yes?"

"Where are you putting the saddle?"

He looked slightly confused. "It's a saddle for one. We cannot both sit astride it, and it will be safer for us to ride bareback. Otherwise, whoever's sat behind the leader will end up sitting too far back, and that could damage her haunches."

"Oh, I see." She eyed the horse warily. Right. So this was happening. "And you can still control her—she's not going to run away or anything?"

This time, Morcant grinned at her, and her pussy clenched. But then his eyes crinkled, and she had to physically restrain herself from jumping him. "You have ridden before, yes?"

"I'd rather mount you than some giant quadruped," she muttered under her breath.

"Pardon?"

Kenna shook her head quickly, "Oh, nothing." She was a dragon now. She was in charge of her own emotions. She felt no fear. But when she walked up to the creature it whinnied, and she took a few hasty steps back. "I've seen other people ride," she offered up.

MORCANT COULDN'T WORK OUT WHAT WAS MORE AMUSING: Kenna's uncertainty about riding a horse; or her determination not to let on about it. He'd never seen a face so expressive and open, and right now it showed that she wasn't sure about this. He was getting a peek beneath her confidence, and he couldn't help but be a little overwhelmed at getting to see this side of her.

"Is there somewhere I can put the saddle, so it doesn't get ruined if it rains?"

Kenna nodded and took it into the forge, clearly eager to get as far away from Steorra as possible. At least it gave him a chance to have a think about how he was going to work this. For a brief moment, he was relieved. Not about her nervousness of course, but rather that focusing on her would distract him from the memories haunting him. Almost. But he wanted to help her, even if it meant facing fears better left to the dark. Perhaps he should start with a simple exchange of names?

When she returned, he encouraged her to stand close. "Why don't I start by introducing her to you?"

Her look of incredulity made him chuckle. "She's more intelligent than you think, I promise."

With a deep breath, Kenna moved closer to the horse and reached out a tentative hand. Steorra gave a gruff huff, and Kenna froze for a second, before flailing her arm behind her towards him. "Morcant," she blurted in a faux-whisper. "Get your arse over here before she chomps on my hand."

He took her hand in his, interlinking their fingers. "You really have had some bad experiences with horses."

She snorted. "Yeah, they don't much like me. I tried my hand at shoeing for a smithy a couple of villages over, and I've never felt so disliked by an entire species. Always stomping on my feet or trying to grab a hold of my elbow with those damn teeth."

He stepped up behind her until her body was only centimetres from his. They weren't even touching and he could feel her body heat. He shoved what he really needed—namely her flushed against him, teasing every inch of him—into a tightly locked boxed in the furthest corner of his mind. There'd be time for that later on, only she was driving his senses wild and—*no*. He forced himself to refocus on the task at hand. "Try copying what I do."

She nodded and watched as he held out his hand, palm upwards, for Steorra to nuzzle. His oldest companion, closer to him in some ways than the rest of the Hunt. The horse who'd carried him through the centuries. "Hello Steorra my sweeting." In leaning forward, his shoulder lined up with

Kenna's and he stifled a sigh as she rocked back into the curvature where his arm met his body, almost nestling into the space that he'd intended on keeping between them.

As if she could tell, she glanced up anxiously, and then relaxed at his answering smile, turning back to watch as Steorra nosed his palm.

"Would an apple help?" She conjured a green one from one of the pockets of the leather jacket that she wore and offered it nervously to the mare. "I had one in the office." But before he could reply, the apple was gone and Kenna laughed as Steorra licked her palm for good measure.

"An apple always helps apparently." Apples hadn't been a thing before he'd joined the Hunt, and from Steorra's clear appreciation, she'd like more of them. He stepped forward to blow gently into her nostrils, and she whinnied softly.

"Why did you do that?" Kenna asked.

"It's how horses show each other affection; how they communicate," he replied. "And it's been—"

"Yes?"

"It's been far too long since I've been able to communicate like that with her." He stroked her forelock gently. "You should try it."

And try it Kenna did, even though she was more skittish than a baby foal. But it created some sort of connection between her and the mare, and no less than ten minutes later, Kenna was comfortable enough to mount Steorra. He gave her a leg up, her shapely rear dangerously close to him for comfort. Temptation, right in front of him. He sighed and upturned a bucket for some makeshift steps, before mounting as well, settling the horse as he did so.

There were a few minutes of adjusting the reins and getting used to being bareback after years of a saddle, before he looked over his shoulder at the woman behind him. "You shouldn't hold onto the reins at the same time as me I'm afraid; it'll confuse her."

"I suppose I'll just have to hold on tight to you then, won't I?" The smile Kenna gave him was full of knowing mischief and he suddenly felt a jolt of life right to his heart. She'd never ridden before while he'd been stuck riding in the hinterlands, and now they were going to get to experience it together. To experience the vitality that came with the air rushing past cheeks, staining faces with a buoyancy he imagined she must have felt whilst flying.

"Hold on as tight as you dare." Her eyes darkened and he could see his longing reflected in her face. "We'll start slow and then, if you trust me, we'll pick up the speed."

"I trust you." The words, quiet but sincere, struck him and he dipped his head to kiss her. Long and slow and tender.

"Good. Let us depart."

CHAPTER 11

⚒⚒⚒

SO horse riding wasn't as great as flying, but it wasn't as bad as she'd expected. She hadn't fallen off, and it wasn't as bumpy as it looked. Kenna was fairly certain this was due to Morcant having some kind of natural riding rhythm that she was benefitting from. She'd scooted as close to him as possible, her arms round his waist and her body moulded against his, so she was able to mimic his rise and fall.

Yeah. Because that was totally the reason she was doing it.

He'd told her to hold on, but after that sweet kiss she'd needed to hold on to something—*someone*—before she did an Arlee and mock-swooned off the damn horse.

She tightened her grip as they soared over a hedge. Goddess that was unnerving. At least when she was flying, she was somewhat in control, and the sky was devoid of rogue tree branches that came out of nowhere. She ducked to avoid one such branch and shuddered. Yeah, she definitely wasn't going to be taking up riding lessons any time soon, but she also understood why he liked it. It reminded her a little of being on the back of a motorbike, the experience of travelling so fast with very little between you and the ground. And then there was the fact that without a saddle, he was primarily navigating using his thighs. Okay, *and* the reins, but his legs were the part of the equation that caught her attention the most. Kenna rested her chin on his shoulder and peeked down at them. Yup, that was one hell of a denimed thigh.

"Is everything alright?" The wind attempted to snatch up his words, but she still felt a shiver across her skin at his voice. She nodded, forcing her eyes up and away from his legs, and turned her mind back to the job in hand.

Rina had given her all the information she had on the Dragon of Bignor Hill, which admittedly hadn't been that much. The odd reference in a book and the vision hadn't given any information other than location. They weren't exactly certain what she was getting herself in for, but Kenna had made up her mind. She'd go in to talk to the dragon on her own.

She had a feeling Morcant wasn't going to like that very much.

Well, tough. She wasn't prepared to jeopardise any information she'd be able to garner from the encounter; it was going to be hard enough as it was. Admittedly, her entire knowledge of dragons had been gleaned from Benedict Cumberbatch's Smaug in the *Hobbit* films. If this creature was anything like that incarnation, she was going to have to navigate through avarice, petulance, and an ego the size of Sussex. She just didn't have time to throw a non-dragon-y, opinionated, stubborn human into that mix.

Kenna smiled suddenly at the memory of the brandished fork. He really was rather sweet, if a little misguided in his attempts to protect her. At least he wasn't overbearing. At no point had he tried to browbeat her or even talk her into doing what he wanted, and he'd actually left when she'd kicked him out of the forge the first time. That had won him some serious brownie points. Perhaps, if she just explained to him that she needed to do this on her own he'd acquiesce, if a little reluctantly.

She leaned her chin onto his shoulder and snuggled in a little bit closer. He briefly squeezed her hand before he got back to ensuring they got to their destination without incident.

Kenna couldn't remember another time when she'd felt so damn soft around someone. It wasn't, she thought, due to his muscles or his looks—although those were certainly not a drawback—but rather to do with the way he met her eyes. At no point had she felt the need to prove herself to him. Every guideline or boundary she'd set out he'd respected, and he certainly didn't seem intimidated by her job, even if he wasn't overly delighted about the whole priestess thing.

Steorra started slowing, and Kenna sat up, loosening her grip. "We here?"

"We're here."

The clearing they'd entered was some way past the farmland that she was used to seeing, beyond the bounds of the local Tunford farms. There were trees around them, and she could see an opening embedded in the curve of the cave in front of them.

She should have been surprised to see the cave. It wasn't as though they were at the foot of a cliff after all, but somehow it felt inviting and perfectly expected, whatever that meant.

"I don't know where you're supposed to go from here." Morcant sounded worried.

Kenna looked at him in surprise. "You're not going to insist on coming with me?"

He continued to look around the clearing as he answered. "Would you let me?"

Her laugh surprised them both. "No. I wouldn't. But that doesn't mean you couldn't offer."

He turned awkwardly on the horse until his eyes met hers. "I'm not a dragon shifter. You are. I'd likely be more a hinderance than a help to you in there; dragons aren't exactly known for their trust in humans. And this way, I can stand guard on the entrance to make sure you don't get sideswiped by someone else."

Kenna was a little startled to realise he knew her better than most people seemed to. He'd put aside his own pride to do what was best for her, even if it meant he wasn't physically standing by her side. *Oh. I can be soft around him.* She could accept his small gestures of affection for what they were, without worrying he'd read it as a shift in power between them. Perhaps he'd prove her wrong later down the line, but she somehow sensed he wouldn't. He respected her decisions. "Thanks, that's…yeah. That makes a lot of sense." She smiled in an attempt to wave the concern from his eyes. "I might be a while, so perhaps come in after me if I'm not back within an hour?"

The smile didn't work, and he looked more than a little confused. "I'm not certain where you think I should go."

"Into the cave. The one just over there?"

He shook his head slightly.

"Oh. You can't see it." That was a little unexpected; if he couldn't, why could she? He was the one who'd been in some kind of hinterland for centuries—not her. She leaned back and dismounted clumsily from Steorra, "Let's see if it helps if you touch it?"

He got down himself, wrapping Steorra's reins over a branch to stop her from wandering off, and then walked over to Kenna. "Lead on."

Kenna walked briskly to the cave entrance, took his hand, and placed his palm on the rocks that made up the archway.

Morcant looked a little startled but nodded. "Let go of my hand, and let's see if it disappears."

She did and was relieved to note his hand didn't fall through the rock or do something similarly disconcerting. She watched as he moved it away and then reached out hesitantly before hitting rock again.

"I have it memorised, I think. I shall just camp out here for a while. An hour, you said?" He glanced upwards towards the sun. "I should be able to approximate that."

Kenna found herself undoing the strap of her watch and then putting it onto his wrist. "Use this. I've got my phone in my pocket, so I can set an alarm and use that." She did up the catch and found her fingers lingering on the strip of skin between his sleeve and the watch strap. She didn't have all that many things a dragon could consider treasure—no jewellery and she doubted a real live dragon would have much use for her smartphone—but this watch…it had been her father's, and she didn't much like the idea of losing it to some ancient creature. It lived on her wrist, in her office drawer when she was forging, or in its box on her bedside table. If she was going to trust it anywhere else, it was on this man's arm.

She looked away and found him staring intently at her. "Be careful with it?" and before he could answer, she leaned in and kissed him, hard. In that moment, lips pressed together in prayer, his hand catching hers, fingers entangled together, she felt all the solidarity she needed. It was more than a kiss; it was a declaration that she knew he was there for her. His strength, shoring up her belief in herself. She pulled back, and then she strode into the cave without a backwards glance.

. . .

THE CAVE WAS DARKER THAN SHE'D EXPECTED. NOT THAT Kenna had a huge amount of experience with wandering around caves. A quick flick through her phone apps found her a torch. Her path newly embrightened, she headed further into the darkness, checking out her surroundings carefully as she went.

The path seemed fairly smooth, as if the rock itself had been worn into submission by continued weathering over many, many years. Kenna sincerely doubted wind or rain would be able to make it uphill, so it was probably made by a large creature moving in and out of the tunnel. She gave a little huff and almost jumped at the small sparks that lit up her breath. She had to hold it together. She couldn't afford to start sparking all over the place. At least until she could find what she was beginning to think of as the real dragon.

That was the real truth of the situation though. Even though she'd shifted earlier, even though she could see the entrance to the dragon's lair when Morcant couldn't, even though she could breathe fire, she still felt like an imposter.

She wasn't the kind of person wild shit like this happened to. She was the one amongst her friends who was most comfortable within her own space: her forge. She knew the exact sound of her hammer hitting newly heated metal and the hiss steel made as she quenched it. She knew how to make the perfect mould for a casting, how to balance function and skill within a piece of art. She knew her place within the village. How everyone saw her. Not quite villager, not quite artist. It was a weird hinterland to occupy, but she occupied it pretty damn well. Was used to it. Add dragon shifter to that resume and she doubted Arlee would be allowed to bring her Year 6 class back to the forge.

In fact, Kenna was beginning to realise that for all her reluctance to have multiple visitors to the forge, she didn't actually want to isolate herself. She liked popping to the pub with the girls. And she might complain about the farmers not always understanding what kind of smith she was, but she actually liked that they saw her work as having purpose. As being useful for them. And even if she didn't like being talked about by the older residents of Tunford, their determination to continuously feed her for weeks after her father's death had meant more to her then she'd cared to admit.

As the path curved to the left and a dim light shone from round the corner, Kenna realised she wasn't certain whether being a dragon was worth the loss of all of that. The acceptance. Her home. Her community. The family she'd found forming around her. No matter what opportunities being a dragon brought, it could never be worth more than this.

CHAPTER 12

THE lair wasn't quite what Kenna had expected. No mounds of gold and jewels piled up as far as the eye could see. It rather looked akin to what could be considered an open plan cavern? She assumed dragons had suffered from Hollywood stereotypes as much as the rest of them. It was, however, lit up, although she couldn't quite determine the light source. The smoothed walls were bathed with a warm glow that gave them a soft yellow colour that made her smile. It wasn't the fierce glow of her forge, but it felt just as welcoming. Just as *right*.

Kenna gently stroked the rock closest to her. The South Downs was on a bed of chalky hills, everyone knew that, but she had never seen chalk so polished. Hadn't even known it was possible. Her gaze followed the swell of the wall 'til it curved to make the ceiling. This space was cavernous indeed. It made her want to stretch out, unfurl wings from her back, and give into the small part inside of her that felt like a caged animal. So much for wanting to be normal.

"It's been many a year since I've had a visitor."

The powerful voice behind her filled the space, and she

wanted to curl up, to hide away. It was too much, too intense, and it threatened to submerge her.

"That must be pretty lonely."

There was a rumble, and from a far corner cloaked with darkness a creature came into the light.

The deep, rich green of their scales caught the reflection of something, and she followed their flow up a large body that reverberated with power. Power which called to Kenna in a way that she didn't really like.

"Wow. You're...big."

Another rumble, and Kenna realised it was laughter. She was pleased to note that little sparks snuffed out the creature's nostrils. So, it wasn't just her who couldn't always control the fire on her breath.

"I suppose I would seem large to a human such as yourself."

She opened her mouth to answer but froze in place as that snout came alarmingly close. "Ummm... there's this thing called personal space... No offense, but you're pretty—oh!"

A particularly large sniff drew her physically closer and then to her knees, until all she could see were teeth and scales as big as her head.

"You're not human," the voice sounded perturbed, *"and yet your form is such that one would assume..."*

Kenna scrambled back up. "I am human, but there was an incident with a goddess. Belisama. And now I can breathe fire and had a whole transforming-into-a-flying-dragon thing earlier. Not as big as you but still very much dragon-shaped, by all accounts."

"I see."

There was what was most definitely an awkward silence, before Kenna decided to take her life in her hands, relatively speaking. "My friend, she's an oracle of sorts, saw a vision of you here, and so I came because I really don't want to be shifting at inopportune moments. I mean, in the forge is fine, but down the post office, or at the pub? It really wouldn't go down very well. I imagine pitchforks might be involved, though you could probably tell me more about that." There was another long pause once she finished her babbling, and she squinted up to see a large eye scrutinising her. "So I came here? For some help? I'm Kenna by the way. And you are?"

The creature looked at her outstretched hand with amusement, but before Kenna could drop it in embarrassment, it rumbled a laugh.

"Well met, Kenna the Dragon Shifter. I am the last of the true wyvern beneath the hill, Leofric."

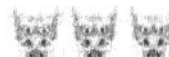

IT HAD BEEN CENTURIES SINCE LEOFRIC HAD LAST SPOKEN TO another creature. Long, silent years kept in their own company.

They'd flown, of course. A wyvern who can't fly might as well curl up and give themselves over the ravages of time. That was certainly how the others had gone. But Leofric had regularly left the safety of the cavern to soar above the chalk hills at night. It had become more dangerous since the establishment of the flying machines just north of the Downs, but they'd not been known as a great tracker for nothing. It had taken a few months to work out the flight paths, and to track their own new route, before getting back into the routine.

They looked down at the female before them who'd mentioned one of the early goddesses. Belisama. That goddess had always approached the Ancients with a certain amount of reverence, though that came from truly understanding the real power behind the flame. But her pantheon had been gone from this realm for centuries. Longer than that even. To return and bestow powers beyond her ken upon this unsuspecting human... it really wasn't quite the done thing.

There was a reason why dragon shifters had had such short lifespans in the past. Their minds, too entrenched in binaries; their bodies, too fragile to cope with regular transformations. A dragon, a wyvern, needed to fly, to be free. And when you took that innate nature and shoved it into a package that was far better suited to the ground and to the mundane, it caused rifts in their minds.

This one though, this Kenna, was staring at them with undisguised interest. Not fear, although they'd sensed a distinct alarm when they'd smelled her earlier. What harm could it do? To share some knowledge with this shifter that might save her some heartache. Save her from herself.

"I will educate you," they announced. "You are the first dragon shifter who ever came to me for advice, and I find that I like it."

"There are others?"

She seemed eager, as if relieved that she was not the only one of her kind. Leofric hated to disavow her of that hope, but it had to be done. "No. As far as I am aware, you are the only one. There has not been a shifter amongst these hills in my most recent memory." They looked down and added, "My most recent memory spanning centuries, you understand."

"Oh." *The shifter sighed, but then straightened again.* "Still, I suppose I have you."

Something akin to protectiveness rose in a wave over them. The shifter would soon find that such things were not simply learnt.

IT WAS BEAUTIFUL OUTSIDE THE CAVE. MORCANT DIDN'T notice it at first; he'd spent so long in motion, that the mere act of stopping and enjoying the weather seemed strangely self-indulgent. But it was. It was absolutely beautiful. He found himself sitting, back against the cave that he couldn't see, drinking in the sunlight. Revelling in the way that the breeze rippled across the grass, caressing each individual blade as the turf curved up and over the hillside.

"What do you think?" he asked Steorra, who was quietly grazing, "Do you think we'll get to enjoy this for much longer?"

Being in the Wild Hunt meant that you were never quite part of this world, always just beyond the Veil of the living, beyond the Veil of the free. And, perhaps unsurprisingly, there'd been a distinct lack of something. No biting wind, no warming sunshine, no sleet to dampen your hands and seep iciness into your very bones. Just a nothing.

Millennia of being just beyond the reach of anything that felt real, that felt alive, had taken its toll on him. On all of those who'd passed through the Hunt. On the brother whose lack he felt even now. No sleep. No rest. Just riding, riding, riding. At the mercy of a capricious god whose idea of sport changed like the winds that never touched them.

And there was a very real likelihood that if he didn't stop Kenna from working on that sculpture, on that piece that seemed to bring her so much joy, they'd be sent back there. Everything they'd been through would have been for not. He shivered, momentarily cast into a shadow of his own devising.

But she wouldn't give up without a fight. He may have only known her for a few glorious hours, but he knew that at least. And the last thing he wanted to do was to fight her.

He wanted to hold her in his arms; make her feel warm and cherished and alive; and draw from her very soul those shallow breaths of desire that had him insensible, as he worshipped every inch of her body.

Ahem.

Morcant gave himself a mental shake. He needed to focus.

Because there was the problem of the goddess. Admittedly, Belisama didn't have the reputation that Nodens did;

although, if he cast his mind back, even Nodens hadn't had a reputation for being as cruel and calculating as he'd turned out to be. That was the true problem with the divine. They listened to no one. They were impulsive and unpredictable; had lived for so long and seen so much that the fleeting lives of humans were but pawns in their wider game. And though Morcant wasn't entirely certain what Belisama's game was just yet, he knew that she had to have one.

But Kenna was far from foolish, and he felt certain that she'd have something fairly biting to say if she thought he was trying to control her. Besides, he really didn't want to. He wanted to be there for her and see her master the powers that she'd been blessed with. To see her shine as he stood to the side, supporting her always.

Perhaps he was wrong?

Perhaps there was a chance, however small that the goddess had plans for good, and that Kenna's life wouldn't get caught up in a forceful rivalry that her body could not withstand. Perhaps, the best thing to do would be to wait.

It went against everything he knew though. After he saw the devastating effects of his brother stepping down from his horse when they first returned from the Otherworld, he swore never to be inactive again.

"Morcant!"

He turned and there she was, striding determinedly over to him, a look of satisfaction on her face that blossomed into a smile when he stood. In an instant nothing mattered other than keeping her safe. Not the Hunt, not Nodens's orders, not even himself. *Nothing.* He'd die to keep her smiling like that. "That was quick."

There was a short laugh, a burst of sound that brought colour to her cheeks as she looked bemused. "Leofric did say that time moved differently in the Otherworld." A panicked hand grabbed at Morcant's heart at that word, until she added, "It feels like I've been gone days." It was okay. She'd come back to him, in this time, in this place. The same woman that she'd been before.

But when she stretched out her arms, he sensed *something* that hadn't been there before. As if she were trying on a new coat she wasn't quite used to yet. She was flexing raw power, and the light in her eyes took his breath away. "So, I'm a dragon shifter," Kenna said, meeting his eyes head on. "And now that I know what the fuck I'm doing, I think I want to have some fun."

CHAPTER 13

THE thing about the South Downs most people didn't quite realise was that it stretched pretty much the entire length of Sussex, from leafy forests to rolling hills, and all the way down to expanses of beach and clifftops that looked over the deep sea. And Kenna longed jump down from Steorra, and instead soar above them where cliff met sea met sky.

Her time with Leofric had left her itching for flight; perhaps it had been being underground, but either way, she'd been tested over and over until the Ancient trusted that she could shimmer 'til she matched the sky. How it worked, she didn't quite know. She wasn't Rina who'd have asked question after question until she understood all the hows and whys and wherefores. And she wasn't Arlee who'd have thrown themself into the learning with gusto. She was her own impatient self, bored mirroring cavern walls and longing to match the glorious blue that beckoned to her.

When Morcant finally slowed Steorra to a walk, Kenna could barely hold herself back from jumping down and shifting straight away. Instead, she checked the stretch of remote cliff for any passers-by who may have wandered a fair way off the standard path.

"I can feel you vibrating with excitement, and my only regret is that I haven't caused that response just yet." His voice, and the low chuckle that accompanied his words, stoked the heat inside her. She leaned forward to kiss his cheek.

"Oh you do, just not quite in the same way."

Another chuckle and her smile was for him as well as the prospect of flying now.

But after he helped her down from Steorra, Kenna paused. "Morcant, I…"

"Yes?"

She bluntly forged forward, not quite meeting his eyes. "Riding naked would be uncomfortable, I assume, for all that Lady Godiva managed it."

"Yes, riding naked would not be very practical."

"So, if I want to 'dragon up'"—her fingers made the air quotes—"then shedding my clothes before shifting probably makes the most sense."

"Probabl— ah. I see. Of course." To Kenna's amusement, Morcant flushed.

"You okay there?"

He cleared his throat. "Yes, I mean… If you'd like to leave your clothes with me, I can certainly watch them whilst you stretch your wings."

Really, Kenna had two options. She could get him to turn around whilst she shimmied quickly out of her things and shifted, or she could let the warmth in those eyes heat up the rest of her. She could feel her face flush as, with a slightly trembling hand—clearly because of the chilly wind and certainly not because his gaze was fixed upon her fingers as she moved—she freed her shirt from her jeans.

He said nothing.

A huff of nervous laughter and she went to turn away, until his touch, barely grazing her wrist, stopped her. "Please, Kenna."

"Please what?"

His voice was reverent, a whispering homage to her. "Please might I…?"

A thrill rushed through her, and she nodded. "Yes, Morcant; yes you may."

It was as if her agreement loosed a whole other tenderness in him. His hand slipped into hers, and he tugged, the movement a question. She answered by turning until she could feel his breath on her neck. His other hand swept her hair to one side, as soft and as gentle as a summer's breeze; she felt his mouth hot against her skin and gasped. This time, it was he who caught at the hem of her top, and tugged it over her head until she stood in the sunlight, all skin and lacy bra.

He fumbled with her bra, cursing under his breath at the "infernal contraption" until she took pity on him and undid it herself, turning round to face him before she let it fall on top of her shirt. More damning silence.

"You did ask for this," she said.

Morcant palmed her breast in his hand and snaked his other arm round to pull her flush against him. "Ask for this?" he murmured, each word burning her skin, "I'd have begged for such a glimpse of this, fȳr, if only your beauty had not stolen my words. I can barely think; you have me so heated with desire for you."

She felt his meaning, twin to her own longing, and kissed him. Short. Hard. Full of promise. His eyes met hers as they parted, mouths open, breathing heavily, searching for something that he clearly found as he said, "Go fly, my fȳr, and when you return, I'll make you soar again."

She took a step back and pivoted to face the sea, before

discarding her jeans and underwear. She flashed a grin at him and ran as fast as she could off the edge of the cliff.

The now familiar burning filled her veins, arms scrabbling, elongating, reforming, as her body reshaped. Wings burst from her back, unfurling before she caught the air current and ascended. One low-flying sweep to reassure Morcant that she was okay, and then she focused on what Leofric had told her. *"When you shift, you are the traces of magic left in the sky and the earth and the sea. You have to acknowledge that, to merge with it, and you will become a part of the landscape that fuels you."*

And they were right. She could feel it at the edges of her consciousness, quivering each time she moved, swooping and soaring. She let it fill her, imbue her very essence with its otherness, and that was it.

She was the magic in the air.

MORCANT FOUND THAT HE RATHER LIKED WAITING FOR Kenna. Once he'd have busied himself with looking after Steorra, but it turned out that she was more stoic about dragon shifters than any horse had right to be, so that left him with nothing to do but put Kenna's clothes in a neat pile and sit back and listen to the sea crash against the cliff. He found it immeasurably relaxing. Besides, when she returned, he had a feeling that he'd need all his energy.

His body was still thrumming with the excitement of being so close to her, of touching her skin and feeling her in his arms. And that moment she'd looked at him over her shoulder, eyes full of mischief and affection, before diving off the cliff, he thought he might expire from wanting her so.

Every now and then he felt her above him, something

slightly different about the way the currents moved and flowed over the cliff. Gods she was beautiful, but it was more than that. She was so full of belief in herself, with a vitality that soothed his jaded soul and made him smile. And hard. He couldn't deny that.

There was a loud thump, and he got to his feet, a little alarmed for her as a part-human, part-dragon red figure shimmered out of the air and bounced across the ground in a manner that couldn't have been comfortable. And then she was there, shaking off scales and running towards him until she leapt into his arms.

He'd been kissed before; centuries previous, and of course by the fiery woman in his arms, but this kiss… If he'd thought her vital before, now she thrummed with life. She was moulded against him, as if she'd sculpted herself to fit with him. Each time he touched her, she became more feverish, more alive, more desperate for him.

And Gods knew he felt the same.

She grabbed his shirt, shucking it over his head, and then they were skin-to-skin, chest-to-chest. If he'd thought earlier that he couldn't be harder, he now found that he certainly could.

"Morcant." Her words stoked his soul, his desire, and he found himself murmuring her name over and over like the words in rituals he'd left behind him long ago. He didn't need deities to worship; he needed her.

He fell to his knees, looking up as her palm gently cupped his face. "Fȳr, let me make you feel as you do me."

Those eyes, bright with longing, darkened as she understood his meaning, and then she nodded, her hands running through his roughly shorn hair, tugging sharply. "Please me Morcant; please my pussy."

"Pussy?" That was not a word he knew or recognised, but

he watched as her hands slipped between her legs and spread pink lips that glistened in the sunlight.

"My pussy."

Oh. Well he could do that.

His hands ran up the back of her legs until they reached her backside, plump and welcoming. He delighted in her squeal as he squeezed, before nudging her until her pussy was in his eyeline. Pink and delicious. He lent forward, his nose nuzzling her, and damn if he didn't almost expire from how good she smelt. Morcant felt her tremble at that. She tensed beneath his hands, and her fists clenched in his hair as she steadied herself.

And then he dove in.

If he'd thought that her scent was intoxicating, her taste sent him reeling. Licking her with wild abandon, each moan and whimper from above sent him deeper and deeper into his need for her.

When his tongue reached her nub, there was a barely muffled groan. He stayed there for a moment, teasing her button before one long swipe across her opening. He took in all that he could of her wet desire for him.

What was the most fun, though, was when he nudged at her opening with a finger as he sucked on her clit. That, almost made her fall over. With his other arm, he anchored her and then slid two fingers inside, discovering new depths, curling and moving until he found that one spot that made her shudder. He felt her gasp then which only urged him on more. Fingers stroking inside her as he teased that nub with regular flicks of his tongue over and over.

He wanted her to come for him. He wanted to feel her let loose beneath his mouth as she had in the skies. He wanted to be the one to make her feel so damn alive again. And he wanted her to know what it was that she had brought him.

Another lick, another gasp and those hands in his hair

pulled his face closer to her pussy as she began almost keening as he hit the right spot, again and again and again.

"That's it. Goddess you're so fucking good at that Morcant. Keep going, just there, there—" her voice cut off as he felt her stiffen against him, and then she was coming. Her pussy spasmed around his fingers; his tongue flooded with the taste of her, her wetness.

It was heady, and he wanted more of it. He wanted to make her come as much as she would let him and to keep going and going until she was had no doubt of her power over him. He went to curl his fingers again, but she was moving away. When he looked at her, ever so slightly confused, she knelt down and reached for his belt.

⁂

SHE WANTED MORE OF THAT DAZED LOOK ON HIS FACE—AND she definitely wanted more of him eating her to an orgasm. The man certainly took pleasure in cunnilingus; that much was obvious from the way his cock was straining against his jeans, but it was also written across his face. He looked drunk. Drunk on her.

Kenna wasn't sure if she'd ever had anyone drunk on her before. It was a fairly heady experience. Made her feel like flying did, and that was headiness itself. But that look, she kind of wanted to have that for herself, not the post-orgasmic haze of delight that she was bouncing off, but the delicious feeling of seeing a lover sated.

He groaned a word she couldn't quite hear as she freed his cock from his jeans. As she took off his jeans, he toppled slightly to the side and laughed that deep throaty chuckle she felt all the way down in her cunt.

She squeezed her thighs together in anticipation, revelling in the pressure against her clit, and then crawled over to him and tossed the clothes aside.

"I want you inside me. Now."

His voice was hoarse as he answered. "Fȳr, I could plead until the end of days, and it still would not express how much I want to be inside you." He sat up and caressed her cheek. "How much I need you. So if you want me, too, then take me. I am yours."

Kenna barely needed the invitation. She pressed at his shoulders and then swung her leg over him with so much enthusiasm that she almost went too far the other side. Pausing to grab at the handbag that lay to his left she swore a little, hands fumbling in her excitement, as she searched until she found her purse.

"Fȳr," he asked as she triumphantly brandished a condom in his direction, "what is this that you're waving at me?"

She laughed as she took it out the wrapper. "Stops me getting pregnant," she said, as she began to slowly, teasingly, roll it down his length.

He nodded in comprehension, but it was that return of that dazed look in his eyes that made her speed it up. She ground against him and was delighted to see him bite his lip. He grabbed her bum again and shifted her forward until each time she squirmed, she was rubbing her clit against the head of his cock.

Fuck.

He might have said that she should take him, but damn if it wasn't mutual. Somehow her plan of riding him into oblivion seemed a little murky and far less important that just having him inside her. Now.

She moaned and shifted so that she could slide down onto him, taking each inch of cock as it filled her so satisfyingly. As she bottomed out, her gasp matched his, and then his hands were on her hips, pleading with her to ride him, to feel that tantalising motion that urged her closer back to that edge.

Ever since she'd first stood naked in front of him and he'd draped his jacket round her shoulders even as he'd undressed her with his eyes, Kenna had expected to want to take her time, to relish this moment. But she hadn't counted on the desperation. The desperation to make him hers.

As they moved together, she arched her back as one of his hands roughly took her nipple between his fingers, rolling it backwards and forwards. And then her voice betrayed her as his other hand darted down and his calloused thumb moved against her clit. It was that, that undid her completely. The rough skin circling and teasing over and over until she found herself at the brink, unable to think past anything but his hands and his cock and those eyes that were fixed on hers.

And there was that word again, "Fȳr, my fȳr," as she tumbled over into a haze of pleasure that sent her as dazed as he'd been. He thrust into her, faster and faster until he too called out, as she had done, in an explosion of desire that she hoped—somewhere in the recesses of her mind—left him as sated as it had her.

"GRASS STAINS AREN'T VERY SEXY IN THEMSELVES," SHE SAID, as they lay by the edge of the cliff, curled up in each other. "But I think that seeing grass stains will make me think of this for a good while."

"Yes, I've never been so grateful to have grass beneath my back."

"Oh!" She sat up. "It wasn't uncomfortable was it?"

He chuckled, and Kenna felt an answering amusement mixed with heat. "I could be sat on the edge of that there cliff, and if I were buried to the hilt in you, it'd be like sitting on clouds."

She rolled her eyes at him and pushed at him playfully. "Oh hush."

"It's true." He sat up next to her. "Although perhaps it would be slightly more circumspect if we didn't share our passion whilst dangling our legs over a cliff edge." He reached to where his jeans lay discarded, and she felt a pang of disappointment. If only they could sit here forever, in this moment of their own making. Although, they probably weren't quite far enough away from the general path for all that.

Steorra whinnied, and Kenna sighed, getting up to grab her own clothes. "This was fun though, right?"

"Fun?" He came to stand behind her, his breath caressing her neck. He wasn't even touching her, and she could still feel the heat between them. "That was far beyond fun, fȳr."

She laughed then; a short abrasive sound that had all her relief bound up in it. It was okay. It wasn't just she who felt like this intensity, this connection between them, had been fucking awesome. He'd loved it too. She turned and kissed him then, sweet and hot in one, before getting dressed. "Have you any plans for this evening?"

"I suppose I should check in with the rest of the Hunt…"

"And I with Rina…"

"Where—"

"What—"

Their words collided and they laughed, letting the tension dissipate. He gestured to her to go first.

"Where are the rest of the Hunt?"

"At the Golden Martlet, an inn towards the centre of the village."

"Oh I know the Martlet, though I've never heard it called an inn before! The pub's where most of the local socialising takes place—Tunford's pretty small—so I've spent a lot of time there since settling in the village." She stopped her babbling with a rueful smile and added, “It’d probably be where I’d choose to meet Rina.”

“So, in that case”—the now fully dressed Morcant leaned in to pressing a kiss to her cheek—“to the pub?”

“To the pub.”

CHAPTER 14

INTERLUDE

THE newcomers seemed set on getting all-out drunk for the second night in a row, all except the woman with them. Tegan had seen Aerten's face when she'd come down to clean the lines that morning, and she had a strong suspicion that she'd be avoiding drinking for a little while. Hopefully that would mean she'd be able to keep the long, dark-haired one under control, and possibly step in if Deuroc continued with what she could only assume were attempts at flirting. It was kind of adorable really, if a little misguided. The last thing she had time for was any kind of dalliance. She had the pub to run and the family stuff to… manage.

But all in all, it seemed like a fairly standard work night. Her regulars were sat at the bar, and Leah was in the kitchen, cooking up a storm as per usual. Cheesy chips, or chips with gravy, fried halloumi sticks, pork scratching, and arancini balls and all that good, hearty pub food that she'd insisted on putting on the menu when she'd taken over from her mum.

The mark-up on fresh food like that was worth Leah's part-time pay check, especially when, after a long day's work, farmers tended to come in and load up on multiple dishes to-go with their pints. Besides, it was probably good for the quiet chef to spend some time outside her tiny cottage; woman seemed scared of her own shadow.

The door opened, and in came Kenna, blazing red hair loose around her shoulders in a manner that Tegan didn't ever remember seeing before. She was laughing at one of the newcomers, the one who'd had other lodgings the previous night, and Tegan had a suspicion that she knew exactly where those lodgings might have been. The blacksmith practically bounded—yes, *bounded*—over to the bar. Sickeningly cheerful.

"Heya, Tegan, two glass of white please. Rina here yet?"

"Not that I've seen—"

The door opened again, and the woman in question strode in and over to the bar, dumping her bag with a thump at her feet, and swinging onto a barstool next to Kenna. She leant back slightly to meet the eyes of the man standing next her friend and gave a curt nod. "Morcant."

He nodded back, more warmly. "I shall leave the two of you to it and shall join my"—his look towards the increasingly raucous table where his friends were sat was a little wide-eyed—"compatriots. Kenna."

"Morcant." She grinned back at him.

Now that was warmth for you. Tegan could have warmed her hands on the sparks between those two.

He leaned down to kiss Kenna's cheek and then walked off as Rina stared at her.

"You're glowing," Rina said, accusatorily.

Kenna frowned. "I'm not glowing."

"Oh yes," said Tegan, leaning across the bar to hand them

their wine, "You are definitely glowing. There's a whole lit-up-from-within thing going on here."

Rina snorted in amusement as the redhead glared at them both. "Really, Tegan? You too?"

"All I'm saying is that *Morcant,*" she said, mimicking Kenna's voice, "didn't stay here last night…"

"Well, he didn't stay at mine!" There was a pause as she reconsidered briefly. "Actually, he did sleep outside the forge, but that's not the point. And even if we had…" Her voice trailed off, and she flushed. "Oh crap, I've gone red, haven't I?"

"The perils of being a redhead," grinned Rina. "I've texted Arlee and once they get here, you can share with us all of the gory details."

CHAPTER 15

MORCANT watched as Kenna and Rina moved to a table in the corner and started talking in hushed tones. He supposed that that was best. Talking about meeting ancient dragons in front of the landlady might be a little much.

"Well. The wanderer returns, complete with conquest."

He tried to resist the urge to growl at Herla, but Aerten stepped in, raising her hand and slapped the king across the back of his head. "A bit of respect, oh mighty leader. For both Morcant and the lass. We wouldn't want anyone to think you were jealous."

His king looked at her and pouted, rubbing the back of his head.

"And at some point, you're going to have to take a break from the quaffing of ale, and actually take a look around you. We are free now. Try and enjoy it instead of being a prize fool, and an annoying one at that."

Herla grumbled good naturedly, but Morcant was struck by her words. Free. They were free. Or at least, they were for now, and that continuing freedom was dependent on him.

He who, not only hadn't prevented Kenna from achieving powers, had actually helped her find the ancient so that she could master them. He pushed away the basket of food in front of him, suddenly feeling very sick.

"You look pale for someone who just kissed a pretty girl."

Sten wasn't looking at him, but there was no mistaking that Norse accent. And Sten speaking was such a rare occasion that when he did speak, you listened.

"That pretty girl is…" he sighed. How to explain it? How to explain the vitality that was Kenna? "She's so alive."

The rest of the table fell silent, and he glanced around. "She is. They all are—can't you feel it? It's that thing, that essence that was missing when we were *there*. I can feel it thrumming through my veins, how alive everything is. It's intoxicating."

"Intoxicating?" Sten took a sip of his drink. "I'm glad you find it intoxicating. Me? It mostly reminds me of how very dead all my loved ones are. That I should have been buried with them."

Deuroc, who'd walked over from where he'd been attempting to engage Tegan in conversation when the lull had fallen across them, rested his hand gently on the Viking's shoulder, his face sombre. "We know. We've all lost those who were ours."

Morcant caught Aerten's eye, and she smiled a bittersweet smile. It was different for the two of them. There had been no one left for them to leave behind in the past. Their only remaining family members, his brother and her sister, had been of the Hunt. Had ridden with them. Had died.

She got up suddenly and took a side door outside.

Herla went to go after her, but Morcant shook his head. "I'll go."

He found her standing outside, the cool breeze coming off the Downs catching the curls of her hair and lifting them, so it looked like they were floating. But her eyes were shuttered, and as he approached, she put out a hand to stop him.

"You feel it, don't you? That responsibility to live."

He nodded.

"When my sister died, when Brianne stepped off her horse into oblivion, I swore I'd get revenge. Revenge on the Gods, revenge on the Romans, revenge on everyone who broke her so. My life is hers; I am her avenger. I don't have time to mourn her or my mother or the mountain of dead that you pulled me from. I have to live, and I have to live doubly for her." Her voice broke, and he sat down on a bench opposite her.

"My brother"—he cleared his throat—"my brother brought me up, took me with him when he learnt to hunt. I learnt alongside him. And when he joined Herla's troop, they took me too. I was one of them because he was one of them."

He turned away and looked over the rolling hills that they'd spent millennia riding across, his hands suddenly clammy. The Hunt had had to hold on to him the day they'd returned. Deuroc had wrapped his arms round Morcant to stop him from dismounting and joining his brother and had held him as he'd wept, confused and angry. So fucking angry. His hands had been clammy then, too, so slick with sweat that the reins in his hands fell, and he'd had to reach down to grasp them once more.

Morcant had been in battles. He'd seen the aftermath of massacres. And nothing had made him feel so hollow as the mass extinction of men who had no concept of their own fate. No bodies left to mourn, just dust.

"He should have been here too. He should be filling that inn with his own effervescence. Instead, it's just me, and I have to somehow persuade a god that we should get to stay. A god who refuses to talk to anyone else, who talks about the Godstouched and magic, and all I want to do is to talk to my brother and ask him. Ask him what it is that I should do, now that I am the one making the decisions."

He felt Aerten sit down beside him. "We will always feel their absence, Morcant. And that is as it should be. It just somehow seems so much crueller, knowing that they could have been here too."

"But what are we to do with that knowledge?" He felt the sharp bite of nails in his palm, and looked down, barely registering the fact that his hands were curled in tight fists.

She was quiet then, unable to give him or herself the answers either of them craved. All they could do was to try and carry the weight of a life unlived alongside their own.

CHAPTER 16

ARLEE'S enthusiasm for seeing Kenna's dragon form had had to be quelled pretty sharpish. Their voice carried at the best of times—Kenna supposed that came from having to manage a mini army of ten-year-olds during the day—and even more so when they got excited. Even an excitedly hushed whisper could carry.

"You've gotta show us, Kenna, please."

"I've already seen it," teased Rina.

Arlee merely stuck their tongue out at the librarian and turned back to Kenna. *"Please."*

She laughed. "It's a pretty large form Arlee; I can't exactly change here. Besides, right now I want to know what's going on."

"What's going on? You can turn into a dragon is what's going on!" Arlee was practically vibrating in their seat, each whisper imbued with awe. *"A dragon."*

"Rina's an Oracle."

"What?" Arlee swivelled to look at Rina, who rolled her eyes and crossed her arms. "What do I get?"

They both stared at Arlee, and they huffed in response.

"Fine. Whatever. I'm too busy with assessments and marking to have to deal with additional woo at the moment anyhow."

Their disappointment was obvious, and Kenna reached over to squeeze their hand. "If it's any consolation, it hasn't been all that great really. A goddess showed up, claimed me as some kind of devotee, granted me dragon-shifting abilities, and then fucked off. And the one time I could have really done with her help? She fucks off again!"

"And don't forget the commission," added in Rina. "The one that she wanted you to work on and that knocked out Mr Dark and Broody over there."

"He's not all that broody; he's actually kind of sweet."

They both looked at her, eyebrows raised, thoroughly sidelined from dragon talk by the prospect of gossip and a potential happily ever after. Kenna sighed. She'd spoken without thinking, but there was no way that they'd leave that comment where it was. She was going to have to give them something. "He's not bossy at all, just kind of hangs back in case I need him. I like that in a guy. I don't need anyone running my life for me."

"Wait, you *like* like him?" Arlee sounded surprised. And Rina looked more than a little bemused at their surprise.

"What, like you haven't noticed them eye-fucking each other every chance they get? I thought she'd burst into flames when he kissed her cheek earlier—and not because of any potential internal dragon combustion."

"There was a kiss?" Arlee looked absolutely delighted. "There's been kissing, Kenna?"

"There's been...kissing."

Big mistake. Huge.

Arlee and Rina swapped glances and then turned on her as one.

"There's definitely been more than kissing—"

"—you've totally been holding out on us—"

"—please tell me there was groping—"

"—look at her face, you really think they just stopped at groping—"

"—fucking? I mean, it's been ages since you've had a good shag—"

"—and now that you're a dragon, with all those pent up flames—"

"—it wouldn't be healthy or even safe—"

"—regular orgasms are clearly going to have to be a priority from now on—"

"—so spill!"

Kenna blinked at the barrage and grinned. "Well, it was kissing at first. Before we went to find the dragon. And then after…well after I went for a fly."

"Went for a fly, yeah, cos that's totally normal," muttered Arlee. "No, no, carry on!" they added, as Rina and Kenna both glared at them. "Don't stop on my behalf, we can talk flying after all the good stuff."

Kenna felt her cheeks heat up and ducked her head, "You know what happens when I shift back Rina, you saw it."

"*Oh…*" the word was drawn out and the brunette laughed, the sound sudden. "You're all giddy from flying, and then there's you all naked in front of a very appreciative man."

"Exactly; you can extrapolate from there, I'm sure." For some reason, Kenna felt rather shy about it all. It had been more than a little special, wildness aside, and she liked that it was their moment, caught between sea and earth and sky and framed by the clouds above.

Arlee smiled and nudged her shoulder gently. "You *like him* like him. That's cute."

"It's…something, for sure."

They grabbed their blazer and stood up. "Well, everyone else has seen this commission in action, so I want to too."

"I've not seen it in action exactly, just the echo left

behind," said Rina as she, too, grabbed her coat and bag and looked expectantly at Kenna.

"Fine," she sighed, but there was a part of her—that fiery, dragon-y, flying part—that felt a frisson of excitement at the prospect of returning to the forge. Returning to those rays of metal that lay on her work bench, calling to her.

TECHNICALLY SHE KNEW THE FORGE WAS QUIET WHEN THE three of them entered, but it didn't seem quiet to her. That calling was louder now, and the palms of Kenna's hands itched.

"You want to work," said Rina in surprise. "But you never work in the evenings if you can help it."

"I never work in the evenings because the two of you told me it was unhealthy to do nothing but work," she retorted, but it was true. She did want to work. To swing the hammer and hear the clang of metal on metal and the hiss of the oil as she quenched each new curved piece. She *longed* to work until she almost felt sick with her inaction. "Ah, fuck it."

She grabbed two pairs of goggles and tossed them over to Arlee and Rina, and then grabbed her own and the gloves from off her table. "Wanna see what I can do with my own flames?"

Rina looked worried, but Arlee almost bounced with excitement. "Fuck yes. Show us what you got, Kenna girl."

A hairband caught unruly curls up and out of her face before she grasped a piece of unburnished copper, held it up to the light, and then sighed with relief as the nausea relented. The copper glinted the way she needed it to. She could see it now, what this piece needed to be, the way it needed to curve and glimmer and become the very essence of light itself, and it was exhilarating. She placed it on the anvil and picked up her hammer and tongs, shifting until they sat in her hand the way she desired them to, opened her mouth, and breathed out.

Flames hit the metal at a concentrated midheat, slowly heating the copper 'til it glowed and then down came her hammer. She barely felt the sweat drip from her brow as she returned the hammer to the metal over and over, turning and sculpting, the flames and light dancing beneath her eyes.

It felt more intense now, working with her own flames. Now that she knew her shifting abilities drew on traces of magic left in the world, she could almost feel the air vibrating, changing, moving around her. There was magic in the air, and it was fuelling her flames and this work. It seemed appropriate, somehow, that this was the case. That it was the air that allowed her to create these rays of light for her goddess.

There was a pressure just behind her eyes each time she put a piece of metal down, so she stopped putting them down. Just kept going, letting the air and the flames and the compulsion drive her.

Over and over she worked, moving between anvil and oil and the worktable, working piece after piece until even the sounds of Arlee and Rina's talk behind her faded into nothingness. All there was, was her and the fire and the copper. Moments blurred into each other as she found herself in a seemingly perpetual cycle of heat and hammer and shape and quench. She dashed sweat from her eyes and continued on.

Behind her, she was dimly aware of some gasps and a squeak that almost certainly came from Arlee, but she pushed those intrusive sounds aside, so that she could focus all that she was on the metal in front of her. She didn't need that right now, she needed to work. She needed to create, needed piles of copper rays shining out at her.

More breaths, more flames, more of that magic, that air, of her being poured into the copper until a cool hand on her forehead jerked her out of her routine and made her take a step back.

"I do not mean for you to burn up with your work."

Belisama stood before her, golden, flaming hands on Kenna's forehead and cupping her cheek. The goddess looked more than a little frustrated.

"I forget how fragile you mortals be."

Kenna blinked at her woozily, and then lost herself in the yellow flames flickering against her forehead, her eyes caught by their dancing beauty. "How?"

"The yellow flame is the coldest part of the fire, and even if it were not, you are indeed my priestess. My flames shall not burn you." The goddess looked over her appraisingly. *"You have shifted, I take it?"*

That brought Kenna a little further back to herself, the anger that flooded her veins washing away some of the frenziedness that she'd been feeling. "Yes. After you abandoned me last time to the shadow god. Don't think that I've forgotten that, by the way, because I most definitely haven't."

"Kenna," murmured Rina nervously, "perhaps we don't get cross with the flaming deity...?"

The goddess turned her look over to her friends, and Kenna stepped in front of them. "No. They are mine."

"And you are mine."

"I am...yours-adjacent. I'm not sure how big a fan I am of all this..." she waved her arms around. Her head spun, and she gasped as her hands opened and her tools dropped to the floor. The sound they made as they hit ripped through her, and she clutched her head, trying to cling onto some semblance of normality. Her knees weakened, and she staggered and probably would have fallen, if Arlee hadn't slipped an arm beneath her to hold her up.

"Fuck, Kenna." They glared at Belisama. "Is this your fault?"

She flared a little, and Kenna whimpered. It was too much. Too much light, too much noise, just …too much.

"You have pushed yourself too far today, and I will not have my priestess falling ill at this point. You should rest, child."

The hand was back on her forehead, and Kenna felt the light flare. It was as like a balm soothing her head, and then it was gone, retreating with the goddess back to the statue in the corner.

"Wait, please." The words felt like treacle on her tongue.

The process of transfiguration that had started already seemed to pause, the figure half-aflame goddess and half-cooling metal sculpture, and it met Kenna's eyes.

"Yes?"

Kenna struggled for a moment to send her thoughts to her mouth, tried out the shape of them with her tongue before saying quietly, "This compulsion to work, to fly, it's so strong. It will abate?"

The figure nodded once, slowly.

"And once I finish this commission, it'll be easier? Things will work better?"

Another nod.

"Okay. I will complete it but after this, please, no more unannounced visits. It's too much."

There was a low chuckle and then the transformation was complete.

Kenna was vaguely aware of Rina wheeling her office chair behind her, Arlee helping her into it, and their voices above her, talking. And then silence.

CHAPTER 17

BY the time it came to closing, Morcant had eaten his fill of what the Golden Martlet had to offer and was contemplating where the five of them would spend the night.

Tegan came over, eyebrow quirked and looked at them. "You guys need board for a second night?"

A round of sheepish acquiescence met her question, and she rolled her eyes. "Fine, same rooms as before. You know the drill. Oh and, Morcant, Rina called. Kenna's apparently exhausted, and she asked if you wouldn't mind holding off on going up to see her. I imagine you'll need to crash on the floor in one of the rooms or sumat."

Morcant was enveloped by an overwhelming feeling of dread. She'd pushed herself too hard, and it was his fault for not stepping in earlier, for not managing to persuade her how dangerous all of this could truly be. He must have had wild eyes to match the sudden racing of his heart because Tegan added kindly, "She said that she's fine, just tired. Let her rest; I'm sure you can tire her out again tomorrow."

There were chuckles at that, and the pounding of his

pulse abated slightly; she was okay. It was okay. He wasn't going to lose her. He took a deep breath and ignored Herla's curious look. "Thank you for the offer of a room, but I feel like sleeping in the fresh air would do me some good."

She paused. "If you're going to sleep outdoors, you've got to be careful where; some of the farmers wouldn't be shy about chasing you off their land if they saw you. Why don't you crash in the pub garden? That way, if it pours, one of the others can let you back in."

That seemed like a decent solution to what was, he realised, actually a bit of a problem. Perhaps it was because these buildings were so different from the ones he'd once inhabited, or perhaps it was because he had become so accustomed to centuries outside, but the thought of sleeping indoors was making him feel more than a little uneasy. And with the shadow of that smothering panic across his chest and lungs, the last thing he wanted was to stay trapped inside. He needed to breathe.

"I'll join you!" announced Herla, only slightly slurring his words. Morcant was sure that he heard Aerten curse under her breath, but his king seemed insistent. "It'll be good for me. Fresh air 'n all that."

Which is how he found himself lying on a grass near the bench he'd sat on earlier, watching Herla try and wrestle a blanket into submission. They'd bundled clothes up for pillows, but Tegan had stubbornly handed them blankets for warmth and almost growled at them when they'd said they'd be okay. Morcant was beginning to see exactly why Deuroc was so taken with her; she had a permanently bemused air and was gruffly protective of them, even if she did find their idiosyncrasies vaguely irritating at times.

"Morcant?"

He stared up at the sky, dark and darned with stars, and

sighed. He really didn't want to deal with Herla's drunken ramblings. "My King?"

Herla practically growled. "Those formalities were dropped centuries ago. Please don't resurrect them now." There was a pause and then he sat up, turning to stare at where Morcant lay. "I know you all think that I'm a fool, drinking the way I have been, but I don't know what to do, how to act in this new world. With this new lease of life. Sten is as silent and uncommunicative as ever, Aerten is angry at the world, and every now and then I see this look of hollowness in Deuroc's eyes. I did that. Through my foolishness. And then there's you."

"Me?"

"You have this weight on your shoulders; this burden that the god has asked you to bear, and it's simply not fair. It should have been me. It should be me." There was a bitterness in his voice that startled Morcant. He supposed that he'd never really considered it that way; his communications with Nodens had been a burden, of course they had, but he'd never thought it anyone's fault but the god's. Certainly not his king's.

When he spoke into the darkness, he tried to make his voice gentle. "You didn't ask for this—none of us did—and this is no more your fault than it is mine. And for better or for worse, you are my king, and you have ridden with us through those barren hinterlands into this moment where the sun kisses our skin and the saltiness of the sea breeze lingers in the air. We survived, and you led us through that."

Herla laughed. It was not a nice laugh. It held anger and resentment and Morcant suddenly saw his king for who he was. A man so completely full of self-loathing. "I? I led you through nothing. Deuroc was the one who prevented you from following your brother; he was the one who found Aerten and Sten. I merely watched as my men died and time played its tricks on us. I held onto our captor, the Hound, and existed. As I still do."

Morcant felt a flash of anger then. They all struggled with it, with their hopelessness; Herla did not have a monopoly on guilt, but when he turned to answer him sharply, a moonbeam illuminated the other man's face, and he saw the tears that silently fell down Herla's cheeks. Angry, silent tears that Morcant knew only too well.

"Perhaps sleep will ease our pain a little?"

The short answering laugh was not unkind. "Perhaps. And perhaps when I wake, I shall do something other than pretend as if I'm not responsible for all of this."

They all had their burdens to bear; whether it was he, trying to find a balance between the Hunt and the woman who'd taken up seemingly permanent residence in his mind, or Herla, mourning his inability to affect the Gods themselves.

ᛤᛤᛤ

KENNA DID NOT NEED MOLLYCODDLING.

She'd woken up at the sounds of clattering in her kitchen, to find herself in her own bed with absolutely no recollection of how she had gotten there. There was a clash and a "fuck that hurt" from down the corridor, and then Rina had popped her head round the door.

"Sorry! Arlee's heading to work, but I'll be in with your breakfast in a minute." And she disappeared before Kenna even had a chance to open her mouth and answer her.

Breakfast in bed was not the norm. When the three of them had lived together at uni, it had been the kind of thing that accompanied a particularly devastating breakup or a birthday. But today was not her birthday, and she was fairly certain that Morcant had every intention of enthusiastically eating her out again in the near future. And that left one option.

Worry.

She didn't like people worrying about her, even if it might have been justified. She'd managed to get through her father's death with minimal fuss, and just because she may have passed out last night due to magical exhaustion by a goddess with a work-ethic complex, she didn't expect to have to deal with any more fuss now.

Trying to explain that to Rina when she was in cooking mode, however, would probably be slightly difficult. She claimed it was an Italian thing, to feed the people you love, but Kenna privately thought that it was the only thing her friend knew what to do when someone she cared about was suffering. That would have explained the multiple different flavours of ice cream she'd made during the aforementioned devastating breakups.

Almost as if summoned, her friend appeared in the doorway with a tray laden down with what smelt like really damn good bacon, and were those fried button mushrooms next to the sausages? Okay, perhaps she could stand a little fuss.

As she tucked in, Rina started talking. "So once you've built up your strength a little, I was thinking how you could come with me to the library today? Take it easy, not overdo it. Your goddess seemed very firm about not burning out. We can have lunch together, go for a walk, spitball ideas for keeping your dragon-side under control…"

It was all very sensible and logical, Kenna had to give her that. Rina was great at sensible and logical.

"Have you had any more visions? Did they suggest this was the best course of action?"

The brunette's mouth tightened. "Right, cos following

those visions totally didn't end up with you passed out in your forge. Do you know how hard it is to carry an unconscious woman up a flight of stairs? I do, cos Arlee and I had to do it, and I have no intention of being put in a situation where that has to happen again."

"But—"

"Now I called Tegan last night and told her to let Morcant know that he could come find you today, but that you needed to rest last night—"

"Stop." Okay, that was too far. As much as she loved her friend, and understood her concern, she didn't need Rina to organise her day, and she certainly didn't need her to organise her love life. She was quite capable of managing that herself, as the two mind-blowingly good orgasms the previous day proved. "I love you, but no. I have my own plans for how today is going to go and *yes*," she continued, speaking through what looked like could be an interruption, "I shall keep you and Arlee in the loop, but I am a grown-ass woman. I do not need this level of hovering."

Rina sat heavily on the end of the bed. "I was doing it again, wasn't I? Overdoing it?"

"It's okay," Kenna reassured her, "I know you, and I know what you meant. But, I know what I need to do, and it's not holding my shifting abilities in an iron clasp—I think that would be far worse. I just need to finish the commission, and I'm going back to Leofric to work out how I can get there."

CHAPTER 18

IT turned out that getting to a dragon the second time round was a little more difficult if you didn't have a horse to ride across the Downs on.

Kenna, laden down with a lunch that Rina had somehow managed to throw together in between applying meticulous makeup and cooking breakfast, found herself wandering along a hedgerow in general direction of Leofric's cave. There was no doubt in her mind about the direction she had to take, which seemed a little odd, but she put down to in built dragon-dar or something.

She could have flown, of course, but that would have meant leaving behind the lunch that Rina had made, and Kenna thought that might have been pushing it a little. If she wouldn't let Rina hover over her, the least she could do was eat the delicious lunch she'd prepared. Plus, there was the whole naked thing. Stripping to transform in the cave itself had been one thing but turning up naked seemed like quite another.

So instead, she got to enjoy the countryside of the South Downs. Fields of crops lay like patchwork over the hills before her. It had been far too long since she'd gone for a walk. Her days seemed so full with work and then trying to socialise so she didn't spend all her time alone. She'd forgotten just how breathtakingly beautiful it could be.

She raised a hand to acknowledge one of the farming locals from the Martlet, who was working his way round the field in a combine. The dust from the discarded chaff floated in the air as she crossed into the next field.

Morcant would like this.

All of a sudden, she was overcome with this longing for him, to walk hand in hand across quiet fields and enjoy the peace of nature. They'd spent so much time moving, rushing from place to place, that the idea of just stopping and being with him, experiencing this with him, made her smile. It took her back to the hush of their post-coital holding, together on the edge of the cliff, with nothing between them and the sky. That quiet, however momentary, had been special.

But there was something about these hills that was powerful too. Her forge was rarely quiet—how could it be with the hammering and flames that were necessary to bend the very essence of metal to her will—but there was something similar in that earthy intensity, to what she felt as she walked along now. Maybe this was what Leofric had spoken of; that awareness of the world around, the awareness of the magic in the air and the earth. It was almost tangible to her. She'd felt it the night before in that compulsion.

There was magic in the metal, magic that needed to be let out, and she was the only one that could release it.

THE CAVE DIDN'T LOOK ANY DIFFERENT THAN IT HAD THE DAY before, but Kenna felt different. Stronger. And when she strode down into its depths, she found herself smiling.

Leofric hadn't been all that surprised to see her return.

"Ah, the shifter returns. And how was the sky, little one?"

And that excitement of speaking to another who understood, who *knew*, came flooding back. "Exhilarating. I've never felt anything like it. Thank you, Leofric."

The rumble that she'd come to recognise as the ancient dragon's chuckle, made the rock beneath her feet vibrate, and she planted herself firmly, so as not to fall over.

"I do have a question though…"

"Another? My, how curious you are. Ask away."

Relief flooded her, and she noticed herself exhale slowly and without any sparks. She'd been so worried that they wouldn't have had the patience for any more questions, but this clearly wasn't the case. "Do you feel the compulsion too? Not just to fly, but to use your power in other ways?"

There was a long silence, and then a dark green snout lowered until the top of her head could just see above Leofric's nostrils into their eyes.

"A compulsion? Hmmm…?"

"Belisama said she didn't want me to burn up."

At those words, the nostrils flared, and Kenna had to steady herself to stop herself from being caught up in the air as they inhaled. *"Deities always think that they know everything. What is it compelling you to do?"*

"To forge, I'm a blacksmith. She has a piece that she wants me to work on, but when I did yesterday, after all the time spent with you and the flying and"—she cut off momentarily, unsure whether fucking in the outdoors would have had an impact on her dragon-ness—"being *intimate* with…well, with a member of the Wild Hunt if you must know, I couldn't stop. All that mattered was using my flames to forge and work the metal, over and over."

"It scared you." Their tone was gentle, for all the depth of its timbre.

"Yes. It scared me."

"Unfortunately, this is what happens when Gods interfere in the lives of mortals. It is not a compulsion that you should feel once this piece is complete. I would recommend that you do so soon, however, because I know not what consistent use of your flames whilst in human form would do to your innards."

"Oh," she sighed, and Kenna suddenly felt the urge to cry. "I'm kinda fucked, aren't I?"

"Fucked is perhaps a slight exaggeration; although if what you said about the Wild Hunt... Does this mean that they've been freed?"

"Yeah, I think so. That's what Morcant said."

"Hmmmm..." They seemed deep in thought. *"Perhaps not all is lost. There was power in the Hunt; if you could somehow harness the potential of their freedom, that would probably keep you stable whilst you finish your work."*

She nodded slowly. Okay, so she kind of had a new plan, which involved harnessing some kind of power. That sounded complicated, but doable? Perhaps? Morcant would be able to tell her, she was sure.

MORCANT AND HERLA HAD SLEPT SURPRISINGLY WELL outside. Perhaps it had been the heart-to-heart, or maybe it was just the relief of being out in the fresh air, but they didn't even wake with the sun. It had taken a rather grumpy Aerten to wake them up. Loudly.

But they were now all sat outside on the benches in the pub garden with sandwiches that Tegan had thrust at them when they'd asked for some water. He thought they must be growing on her, because she'd even smiled at Deuroc's flirtatious greeting, and the rolling of her eyes was beginning to seem a little less sarcastic and a little more bemused.

They ate in relative silence, their hunger taking first priority, and then Aerten spoke up. "You know we can't do this forever."

"What?" Deuroc asked. "Eat sandwiches?"

"Stay here, no matter how taken with the landlady you are."

The blond man huffed, but Herla inclined his head slowly. "Aerten is right. If we are to stay, we need to make plans. Plans for actual accommodation and for ways to spend our days that isn't just drinking and eating."

An awkward silence descended, and Morcant realised that they were all very studiously not looking in his direction. *Oh.*

"I suppose, if that's the case, then I should probably have a word with *him*."

Deuroc looked over apologetically. "Aerten's right; we can't keep taking advantage of Tegan's good nature, and at some point, the coins he gave us will run out. We need to know what we're doing next."

There was a pause before Herla said softly, "Your lass… is she the Godstouched that the god spoke of?"

Morcant was the one not looking at them now. He lifted his hand to take a bite of his sandwich in an attempt to give himself a moment or two longer to reply. It trembled, and he let it fall back down to his lap.

"Morca—"

"Yes. Yes, she is" He stood up and began pacing. "She is full of magic that is both her own and not her own and has been recruited by another of the Gods, but she is so *alive*."

"So are we." The Viking's words felt like stones hurled at his body. Each syllable thudded against him. "This is what you all keep saying, yes, that we have a chance to live?"

"Yes." Morcant sat down heavily opposite them and sighed. "I can't stop her—I couldn't stop her—from developing magic. She already had it by the time I met her, but I couldn't let it destroy her either."

Aerten knelt in front of him and forced him to meet her eyes. "No one is asking you to do so. but we are in a hinterland of another type now, and as long as it continues, our future remains uncertain."

He closed his eyes and forced each dreaded word from his lips. "Oh God of the Hunt. God of Dogs. God of the Sea and of Healing, come to us now." And then he waited.

The stillness made the waiting worse. He'd never spoken to Nodens in front of the others before, dreaded the moments when he'd been plucked, unwilling, to communicate with the god. Only this time was worse. This time would decide their fate.

But when the shimmer came, the mixture of light and shadow dancing across the black of his eyelids, he wasn't the only one who saw it. There was a stifled curse from Herla and what sounded like "streð mik" from Sten.

When he opened his eyes, all of the Hunt were staring in consternation at the god. Aerten muttered something about "peacocking" under her breath, and the god himself looked a little disconcerted at the fact that all five of them could see him, although that didn't prevent him from rounding on Morcant and firing vitriol at him. *"You dare summon me, you who are earg?"*

Herla stood at that and cleared his throat. It must have taken all his strength not to take a step back when Nodens whirled around, sending his shadows snaking up to twine themselves round the lower half of the king's body. "I would rather you addressed me, than one of my men. If it's all the same to you."

"If it's all the same to me? And why should I speak to you? Look at the remnants of your men. Two left of your original court, and two strays you managed to pick up along the way. No, I know you

can't get things done. And Morcant has been so good at basic communication even if"—and here the god seemed to swell with rage— *"he seems incapable of stopping some Godstouched whose life spans minutes in comparison to yours. I should end her myself."*

Shadows swum before Morcant's eyes, and he reached out to steady himself. No. No. He couldn't. He wouldn't let him.

Before he could open his mouth to speak, Aerten interjected, "We will see this through; her magic will not a problem for much longer. Ending will not be necessary."

That gaze shifted to her, and Morcant realised in horror that perhaps this was the only way: culling Kenna's magic to keep her safe. The mere thought of it was agony. She would suffer, he knew that much. He'd seen those severed from magic before. It was not something anyone survived without deep emotional scarring. To see his fȳr, his *love,* suffer like that would be too much to bear. He had to say something, to protest, to—

Deuroc draped an immovable arm about Morcant's neck and muttered in his ear, "Not a word. Trust in us; trust in the Hunt."

He'd spent millennia with them. Centuries riding side by side with these companions, and as Herla looked at him out of the corner of his eye, and Aerten's hands remained tightly clenched by her sides, and Sten, of all people, dropped him a surreptitious wink, he realised that he did trust them still. And so, he sat and listened whilst Aerten outlined a plan to drain the woman he loved of her magic.

CHAPTER 19

"I would rather die than let another innocent get caught up in this scitte." Aerten spat the words out as soon as Nodens had left. They were all drained; all exhausted by what had befallen them, but they were all looking at Morcant with more than a little awe. "Fuck, Morcant, you dealt with that pissant on your own all of these years. I'm so sorry."

He looked at her. "We're not going to—"

"Of course not!" Deuroc's arm had loosened round his shoulders now that Morcant wasn't in any danger of launching himself in panic and desperation at a god, and his friend actually ruffled his hair. "We'll come up with a plan, but no. Your lass will be okay."

"Kenna; her name is Kenna."

They all nodded, and for the first time, he felt as if a weight had been lifted from his shoulders. They would find a solution together; it wasn't all on him. Thank the Gods.

"I would like to point out, however," said Aerten, "that you appear to have done very little to actually court her."

"Of course I—" he stopped. Shit, he really hadn't. He'd

helped her find a dragon, and he'd attempted to protect her forge with an eating implement, of all things, and he'd made her come more than once, but actual courting… "I should fix that. What do women these days like?"

"I can help with that," suggested Deuroc. He looked vaguely aggrieved as they all burst out laughing. "What?"

"You need a little help yourself," explained Herla. "Sure, Tegan likes you, but that's more because you amuse her than anything. Morcant, how about gifts? Flowers, jewels?"

"Flowers and jewels are commonplace," Aerten said. "You want something that's going to really make you stand out."

They waited for her to continue, and she just shrugged. "No, that's really all I've got. No-one said I was actually any good at this."

"What do you want to show her?" asked Sten quietly.

Well, that was a question indeed. He supposed he wanted to show her how much she meant to him, and all the flowers and jewels in the world wouldn't be able to capture that. Plus, he didn't really think that she'd be all that bothered by gifts like that. They'd be nice, sure but he'd get a polite smile and he didn't want polite; he wanted joy. And not *that* kind of joy, though that kind of joy was more than a little delightful.

"I'll take her to the beach."

Herla grinned. "That's a great idea! You'll need food and a blanket to cosy up on, and then you can take her in your arms and—"

"Yes, thank you," Morcant said. But Herla was right, food and a blanket, and a moment of their making. She seemed to like moments.

"And we'll stay here," said Deuroc, "and plot. We're good at plotting."

He looked past his friend to where Aerten stood, and she nodded. "Please don't worry; we can take this burden for a time, whilst you focus on not bungling this thing you have with the blacksmith."

⚒⚒⚒

WHEN KENNA ARRIVED AT THE MARTLET, MORCANT WAS out front, clearly waiting for her.

"Hey, fȳr, how was your rest?"

"My—? Oh yes, my rest! I slept well last night, though that might have been in no small part due to the whole almost burning out and fainting thing."

His eyes went wide with concern, and he reached out to tug her close to him. "You fainted? Fȳr, you must take care not to burn so bright."

Kenna met his unwavering gaze and felt her cheeks flush as his hands settled in the curve of her back. "I'm fine, really. I spoke to the dragon, and I have a whole plan of action—though I may need to speak to the whole Hunt about it."

Almost as if summoned, Deuroc's head popped out of the pub door. "Can it wait until the morrow?"

"I mean, it can…"

"Marvellous!" He shoved a basket into Morcant's hands with a significant look. Morcant closed his eyes, as if praying for patience, and then glared at him and shoved him back inside. It was highly entertaining. There'd clearly been a whole plan laid out, if Sten leading Steorra over to them was anything to go by, and for some reason Deuroc had set it all off early.

Her dark-haired man sighed and turned to her. "I had planned on asking if you would like to take a ride this evening, but your plan of action is far more important, especially if it will prevent you from fainting again. This can wait until another day."

But when he went to put down the basket, Kenna felt a jolt of disappointment. She'd lasted this long, and she hadn't exactly exerted herself today, other than go for a walk. Him wanting to go for a ride with her, she instinctively knew wasn't about sex, but rather more akin to the feeling she'd had earlier whilst walking in the fields. He wanted to spend time with her, and there was nothing she wanted more—not even to work on the piece for Belisama. "Please, I've had a very unstrenuous day and feel absolutely fine. Plans of action can easily be left for tomorrow." She placed a hand on his arm, and then continued, quieter, so as not to be overheard by whichever Hunt member was lurking around a corner, "I'd rather spend this evening with you."

So they mounted, the basket tied to Steorra's saddle, and off they rode.

She didn't recognise where they were going at first, Morcant urging Steorra across fields beyond Tunford, but soon she heard the sea.

The thing Kenna loved about the coast by the Downs, is that it wasn't that perfect sandy blanket. It was rough and stony and that wasn't the sound of waves, but rather pebbles being dragged back and forth on the shore. He hadn't brought her somewhere busy, like the bustling crowds on a Brighton shore, but to a smaller one where the shingled beach seemed hidden away.

Grass met pebbles met sea, and they drew up at the edge of the stones, so as not to get stones caught in Steorra's hooves. He pulled out a blanket from the basket and indicated to her to sit down.

For a while, that was all they did. Just sat quietly next to each other, her arms clasped around her knees, her back leaning against his chest, and listened. The ebb and flow of the waves, lapping against the beach was calming. Relaxing. And she could feel it here too, that something just beyond her ken that made her senses tingle. It was the movement of the waves that seemed to be imbued with magic, as if, if she reached out, she'd be able to catch it like quicksilver in her hand.

"I love the sea," she murmured. "But why here?"

Morcant smiled at her. "Because this is my space, just as the forge is yours. When you spend millennia riding through other people's lives, never able to quite reach through to them, you need a space. And whenever the Hunt returned to this part of the world, I'd retreat here."

A wave of protectiveness came over, as strong as any of wave on the beach before them. "This was your escape."

"This was my escape." His arms were warm around her, and as he pulled her close the two of them, he and her, slotted together like pieces made to fit next to each other. "There was so much that we lost in the Hunt. It was as if there were a veil between us and sensation. No taste. No smell. Nothing to touch but the reins of your horse. No weather could touch us, and even the colours of the world seemed muted. But sound…"

He scanned the horizon, and there was that smile again, dancing across his face, "When everything else is taken away, what is left becomes sharper. I would sit on Steorra, at the edge of this beach, and listen to the waves for hours."

She leaned up and kissed his cheek, the bristles of his beard prickly against her lips. "Thank you for sharing it with me."

IT WAS AT KENNA'S URGING THAT MORCANT SHUCKED OFF HIS shoes and socks, rolled up his jeans, and finally made his pilgrimage to the sea. The stones were more uneven than he'd imagined, sharp and smooth edges cold against the soles of his feet, but it was when he stood at the waves edge that he truly took a breath.

This was what he'd dreamed of for centuries. The ability to stand here and feel that tang of salt on the air, to experience the rush of the waves about his ankles. To truly appreciate all that had been beyond his reach for so long.

He felt her hand slip into his, and when he looked at her, she was glowing. He knew it was the placement of the sun behind her and not actually any magical reason, but it seemed like magic. As if the sun itself had seen how full of light she was and was crowning her fiery tumble of hair with its own fiery crown in response.

Morcant kissed her then, and her heated response made him want to melt against her. He could feel her smile, feel his own, and then, laughing, she dragged her mouth away and pulled him into the water.

By the Gods it was cold. Colder than anything he'd experienced since they'd been freed, and it took his damn breath away almost as much as she did. And it wasn't comfortable, somehow his imagination hadn't quite stretched to the discomfort of standing on misshapen pebbles and stones, but as he stood there, he began to feel it. The draw of the waves. Smaller pebbles and stones lifted with each swell of the tide, dragged, and moved until they settled round his feet. And then again and again, until he couldn't see his toes for the pebbles encasing them.

He laughed, the sound shattering the peace of the waves, and he realised that he'd never made a sound here before. He'd always come and sat at the edge of the beach, watching, yearning, but never quite part of the thing he longed for the most. And now? Now he was laughing.

A splash to his right, and he ducked as Kenna straightened, sending a shower of droplets over him. He shook his head and then took off after her, the two of them galloping unwieldly down the deserted beach, mirth spilling out and merging with that dependable sound of the waves.

When he caught her, she slipped her arms round his neck and kissed him. Hard. And there was the moment, caught and captured for his memory to hold onto forever. Her, warm comfort in his arms, her lips soft and supple against his, and that little noise she made at the back of her throat when he did something that pleased her. He wanted to always please her.

They drew apart and rested their foreheads against one another.

"I have food," he offered.

"Food is good." He could hear the smile in her voice as they walked towards the blanket on the beach.

There was a veritable smorgasbord of picnic foods in the basket waiting for them. Tegan had refused to let anyone go and speak to her chef, explaining that Leah "was shy enough, without having a troop of ruffians descend on her kitchen," but had returned with the promise of a basket and a warning glance for Morcant that indicated that he had better make sure that Kenna was happy with it.

And happy she was. They both were. It felt as if nothing in the world could touch them.

CHAPTER 20

⚒⚒⚒

"WOULD you like to stay at mine tonight?"

Morcant looked more surprised at the invitation than she'd have imagined someone who'd eaten her out would be.

"You don't have to," she hurriedly added, not wanting to push him outside the bounds of comfort, but he was shaking his head and smiling.

"I'd love to, Kenna, of course I would."

"But?"

"I…I haven't slept inside a building in millennia. Even before the Hunt, I was more likely to sleep outside, and I don't know how I'd like it. But I want to stay with you." He looked troubled, and she wanted to reach up and brush the worry lines from his forehead.

"It's okay; why don't we start by spending some time together at mine first." She knew she was grinning at that, and by the flush of his cheeks, he was eager to take her up on the suggestion. "And then we can see how you feel when it comes to going to sleep? I live above the forge, but there's grass all around the building, if you need to sleep outside."

His look of relief was a little rueful. "Thank you, I cannot express how much I appreciate your understanding."

She leaned in and kissed him. "And we don't have to go to sleep for a good time yet."

He kissed her back with enthusiasm, and she couldn't help but smile—as if it was drawn, unbidden to her face—as they packed the picnic away.

The ride back to the forge was quiet, the two of them in a comfortable silence that Kenna rarely felt with anyone else. When they arrived, she averted her eyes from the door behind which her tools lay. She was so determinedly ignoring their call that she almost jumped when Morcant slipped his hand into hers.

"Are you okay, fȳr?"

"Yes," she answered, brusquely giving herself a mental dressing down. It could all wait until tomorrow. Tonight, she wanted to kiss every inch of her Morcant's body and let him kiss every inch of hers. The sparks between them were the only fire that she was remotely interested in tonight.

They took the stairs up to the flat over the adjacent garage. It wasn't large, but she'd made it home. A small cosy living room, a bathroom with a power shower to die for, a kitchen which had just enough cupboard space, and her bedroom. That was where she led Morcant now.

The room itself was pretty much all bed, with built in wardrobes at the side, and he looked a little taken aback at the expanse of duvet-covered mattress. Kenna wasn't really a pastel girl, so her sheets were a dark purple, and she couldn't help but imagine how they'd look entangled atop them.

Grinning, she bounced onto the bed and looked at him. "It's comfy, I promise."

She watched as he sat slowly, gingerly, his eyebrows raising as the mattress dipped beneath his weight. "This is indeed comfy, fȳr."

"Wait 'til you try the pillows!" She leaned back until her head sunk amongst the soft fabric, and beckoned him towards her, but instead of coming to lie next to her, he made his way up her body until his face aligned with hers.

"I could try the pillows," he agreed, "or might I, please, kiss you?"

She nodded. And fine, yes, she'd much rather he kiss her than try out the pillows. Especially when he was kissing her like this. Teasing mouth, thigh cautiously nudging her legs open, cock hard beneath his jeans and always with this intense connection. One arm kept him braced above her, so he didn't crush her, until she slipped both arms around him and pulled him down. She wanted to feel the weight of his body against hers, and when he lifted his head in question she said, teasingly, "I didn't say you could stop kissing me."

So he didn't. She didn't know how long they lay there, intertwined, fully clothed, just losing each other in long, languid kisses that made her head woozy with desire. When she finally couldn't take it any longer, she took his hand and guided it beneath her shirt, before almost shoving him off her so she could take it off quicker.

"You seem in some kind of hurry fȳr."

His eyes were filled with bemusement, and that amusement turned to full out laughter when she answered, "I don't know what you're laughing about; the sooner you take yours off, the sooner you get to feel my skin against yours."

That shut him up pretty quick, and he managed to shed his top almost as fast as she did. They both raced to take off trousers, which ended with a gurgle of laughter and Morcant flinging a rogue sock that had got stuck halfway across the room. And then they were naked, and he was looking at her. Really looking at her.

Kenna knew that he'd done this before, when she'd stripped before shifting, and that he'd seen her after, naked above him as he made her come, but somehow, here in her room, it felt more intimate. Like he wasn't just looking at her. Like he was seeing her. He saw the fiery badass smith and the dragon and her body, but he also saw the woman who would walk for hours across the Downs and paddle in the sea. The woman who'd do anything for her friends and whose art meant the world to her.

He saw into her soul.

It sounded ridiculous, but it was true, and it made her feel so very, very exposed. Kenna found herself getting terribly shy, wanting to turn away from his gaze and hide under the covers, but he caught her hand as she moved.

"Why?"

"'Why?'" She didn't know what he was asking of her.

"Why do you turn away when I look at you? You are magnificent."

She laughed, a brittle sound that screamed vulnerability. "Let's put my magnificence to one side for a moment—though truer words have never been spoken—for honesty. You see me. All of me. And that's scary."

He reached for her, and for the first time, she let *her* body relax into *his*, let herself drop her guards for a moment and simply be held. He had one arm around her waist, but it was the one that cradled her head that undid her. He held her like she was the most precious thing he'd ever handled. He made her, the blacksmith with muscles to match, feel delicate.

"I love you," he murmured against her hair, and she should feel scared or shocked, but she didn't. She felt loved.

THIS TIME WHEN MORCANT KISSED HER, SHE DIDN'T HOLD anything back. He felt the shift in her body and in the way she put everything into the clinch. Everything. Before, he'd been amazed by how alive she seemed, but this time it was her passion for life itself that made the kiss.

It was her. No holds barred.

Kenna pushed at him until he fell back onto the softest material he'd ever felt beneath his head and climbed on top of him so she could kiss him some more. She urged his hands to touch her, and he did, caressing and stroking the contours and curves of her body, making note of each movement that made her squirm or make that little moan in the back of her throat.

She was wet too. He could feel it every time she ground against him and it was driving him wild. It was driving his cock wild. Even the slightest sound she made, the smallest whimper, made him harder, and there were lots and lots of whimpers. He reached down to stroke her, slipped his hand between her legs to that apex of heaven, and found her dripping for him. One, two, three brushes against her clit, and she was gone, that quick movement where one second she was above him and the next she was—oh. *Oh.* That's where she was.

He looked down his body as she took a band from her wrist and caught her hair up in it, up and away from where it had been spilling over his torso, and met his eyes with a mischievous wink.

"Be a good lad, and lie back for me. If you don't mind, that is."

Of course he didn't mind! How could anyone object to this, her mouth suddenly hot and wet around his cock; it was all he could do not to buck up into it. She glanced at him, halfway down his length, and her eyes crinkled as she smiled. Then she was going down, down, down until he could feel himself hitting Kenna's throat. Gods that felt good. As she began to bob her head up and down, each movement slick and smooth, he moaned himself. Found himself muttering almost incoherently as she worked his length.

She reached out and held his hand, and that one small action grounded him and made his balls tighten. He gripped the covers of the bed in his other hand in an attempt to claw back some self-control. "Gods, fȳr, I'm so close to coming."

Kenna lifted her head from his cock, and he groaned at the sight of her lips, glistening wet. "Good." Her tongue darted out and swiped the pre-come from the tip of his cock, and he jerked upwards.

With the little self-restraint he had left, he held off from spilling across her, leaned down, and pulled her up his body. Her full breasts were flush against him, and he ran his hands down to her backside before rolling the two of them over until she lay beneath him.

"Good, eh? You want me to come, fȳr?" He nudged at her entrance with his cock, and she arched up, desperation painted across her face. "How about you? What else do you want?" She moaned as he dragged his cock up and across her clit in long, tantalising strokes. "Come, fȳr, what is it that you want? What is it that you need?"

"You," she gasped out as she reached for him, and he felt that all the way down in his toes. Him; she needed him. And he would give her all of him in return.

⚒⚒⚒

AS SHE SPOKE, KENNA KNEW WHAT SHE WAS SAYING. WHAT SHE meant. She needed his delight in bringing her pleasure, she needed the way those kind eyes turned heavy with desire when he looked at her, and she needed the way he filled her up so completely.

Trying to grab a condom from a drawer in her bedside

table was infinitely more difficult when Morcant didn't move his cock from teasing her clit. She found herself unable to look away, their eyes fixed on each other, even as she undid the wrapper with trembling fingers. Then he'd taken it, put it on, leant down, and kissed her with such tenderness.

When he slid into her, it was so deliberate, his eyes so focused on her face, that it had her arching up against him and her eyes rolling back into her head in pleasure. And then he began to really move. Steady, long thrusts that had her gasping and moaning beneath him.

Morcant reached for her hand and then urged it southwards between her legs. "Please, Kenna, fȳr, show me. I want to know how best to please you."

Her fingers moved slowly at first, running between her slick folds and caressing his hard cock as it slid in and out of her, before moving up to tease her clit, circling around the nub in tight movements that synced with his thrusts.

He went to lean back to watch her, and she lifted her leg until it was over his shoulder. A firm hand encircled her ankle and lifted her other leg, and Goddess if his cock wasn't hitting her in all the right spots. Now his thrusts became more urgent, his eyes flying between her legs and her hands rubbing desperately. When Kenna lifted her fingers to lick her wetness off them, he swore. "Fuck. Don't you taste good, fȳr?"

The tang of her taste on her tongue, the wetness that coated her calloused fingers, made her moan, and he reached down to cup her neck, his fingers tracing a path from her collarbone up to her lips. She met his eyes then, staring at him daringly, lewdly fucking her mouth with her own fingers until he could bear it no longer. He grabbed her hand and shoving it back down between them.

"I need to feel you come. I need that, Kenna. Fȳr. Please."

Her fingers echoed his frenzied thrusts, and she let herself float in that delicious haze of lust that descends when on the edge, where nothing matters but being in the present. The feel of his cock filling her pussy, electrifying her nerve endings; the slickness between her fingers that ran down the cleft of her arse until she was completely and utterly drenched; the pressure building behind her clit until she could feel it in the very tips of her toes. Even the sounds they made together were pushing her closer and closer to that final torrent of pleasure. That slap of bodies moving together, the sheen of sweat on his skin, and his eyes. His eyes that remained on hers as she hurtled towards…

And then she was coming, her pussy clenching and unclenching rapidly as her mouth opened in a silent *o* of pleasure, the intensity of the sensations ripping away her voice.

She was vaguely aware of Morcant's muffled cry, and then he was gathering her in his arms even as he drove into her over and over in feverish movements that had her gasping for air until he too, unravelled before her.

He dropped his head on her shoulder, tongue darting out to lick that spot on her nape that made her moan, and he buried his face there, in the curve of her neck and quietened.

I love you too.

THEY LAY THERE FOR A WHILE, AND MORCANT WAS beginning to see the benefits of fucking on a mattress of this softness, as opposed to on the ground, even if said ground was covered in turf. It was comfortable. And you didn't have to worry about protecting your lover's head because, pillows. He could get used to this.

And he could get used to seeing Kenna like this. She was

all misty-eyed and had this lazy satisfied smile on her face that he delighted in knowing that he had some part in putting there. He curled on his side, and she moved behind him, wrapping those arms about him until he was pulled tight into her body, his legs bending at the knee and curling round to mimic hers.

As she wriggled a little to get comfy and slipped her hand up to anchor in his, he felt an ache. This was everything. He was hers and he'd be damned if he'd let anyone, deity or not, change even a single thing about her.

"Morcant?" Her voice was dreamy.

"Yes, fȳr?"

"I have spare blankets if you want to go outside? Only, if we snuggle like this much more, I'll probably drift off."

He paused for a moment, waiting for the panic to rear its ugly head and take control of his pulse and his mind. Nothing. Just the warmth of contentment. "I'd rather stay here with you, if you don't mind?"

She sighed serenely. "I don't mind, that sounds wonderful."

There was some more wriggling, so that they could work the duvet out from under them, and then they were enveloped in the lightest down. *Snuggling was a good word for it.* It encapsulated that feeling of being safe and warm and cosy, just shared. Her breathing evened out and little snuffly snores started emanating from his love.

Sharing moments like this was what he wanted. More than the sex and the physical contact, although he would really like it if that continued also, he wanted to spend time with Kenna. Go to sleep within her arms at night and wake up next to her in the morning. She made his life brighter.

Maybe that was why he found himself slowly relax, the tension of the last few days—even the last few centuries—releasing until he pulled her close and his head rested on the pillow next to hers. His breathing began to fall apace with hers, echoing each in-and-out breath, albeit with decidedly less noise. He finally allowed himself to let go of the tight hold he had on the world around him and drift into a dreamless sleep.

CHAPTER 21

WHEN Kenna woke up, sun streaming in through the window, the space in the bed next to her felt empty. There was a split second of 'What the fuck, where the hell is he?' running through her brain, before she realised that he was sitting at the end of the bed.

She sat up, blinking blearily, and leant forward, running her hand over the contours of his back. "Morcant? Is everything okay?" And then, "Oh shit, was it the sleeping indoors thing? Did it—"

"It's okay, fȳr, I'm okay, I just…" He paused and turned his head away from her. "I need to tell you something."

Her traitorous heart started thudding until all she could hear was blood pounding in her ears. 'I need to tell you something' never boded well. In her experience it implied the loss of funding, the presence of a class of ten-year-olds in her forge, or in one particularly enraging case, the existence of a secret girlfriend. Her fingers twitched, and she almost wished for the comforting weight of her hammer in her palm. "Okay. Tell me then."

His words blurted out in a torrent, "We were trapped in

the Hunt for so many years, and then we were free. Only Nodens, the god who trapped us, said that I had to stop the Godstouched or we'd be sent back, and that's you. Only you're *you,* and you were already working with the goddess, and then you were a dragon, and I couldn't exactly leave you to face being a dragon on your own. And now he's found out, and he wants to stop you, and I don't know what that means, but the Hunt have a plan and—"

She held up a hand to halt the onslaught so that she could process what he'd been saying and also so he didn't pass out from lack of oxygen. That was a whole lot of words right there. "Morcant, look at me."

He did, his eyes anxiously searching her face.

"So, you're being fucked about by a god as well?"

He nodded. "I know I should have told you earlier only—"

She held up her hand again, and he stopped, looking even more nervous if that were possible. "Well if you had, we could have come up with a plan of action together, instead of you beating yourself up about this whole thing." She leaned forward and kissed his cheek. The poor man looked terrified, as if she'd start breathing flames all over the place.

"You're not angry?" His tone was one of disbelief, and she realised that he truly didn't understand how she felt about the whole thing.

"Morcant, you were trapped in the Wild Hunt for centuries by a *god.* A god who was cruel and abusive and who was blackmailing you to do what he wanted, with the threat of entrapping you again held over your head. He's an arsehole, and you're not responsible for his actions."

He fell silent, and she realised that tears were silently crawling down his cheeks.

"Oh love." The words were out before she could stop them, and she moved towards him, taking his face in her hands and speaking fiercely. "How could I possibly be angry with you for this? It's not your fault. If I ever get my hands on your god, however, I'll shatter his head with my hammer."

He bent his head, resting it on her shoulder, and she wrapped her arms around him as his body silently shook with tears that had lain unshed for two thousand years. She held on tightly, blinking the tears away that threatened to well over, so furious and so sad for all those years he'd suffered.

Kenna wasn't naturally an angry person, despite the assumptions that people made when they saw her in the midst of a particularly physical bit of forging, but this feeling? This was cold fury. She would do everything in her power, use everything at her disposal to stop this Nodens from taking away her Morcant, even if that meant asking Belisama herself for help.

THEY ALL GATHERED IN HER FORGE. ALL FIVE MEMBERS OF the Hunt, Arlee and Rina, and Kenna. Morcant had introduced his companions first: Aerten, the only woman in the Hunt, who seemed almost as angry as Kenna felt; Deuroc, the one who'd kept trying to flirt with Tegan; Sten hadn't even spoken, just nodded; and then their king, Herla. Plus, their unofficial member, the Hound, he seemed more than content to ignore any outstretched hand in favour of a jumper she'd tossed in a corner of the forge.

She'd done the honours for Rina and Arlee, making sure to lay emphasis on the latter's pronouns. The Hunt had nodded, almost as one, but she was pleased to note that when any of them addressed Arlee, they used they/them, even if they paused for a moment beforehand to make sure they got it right.

And then it was down to business.

The Hunt had clearly been trying to come up with a plan

of some kind, albeit with limited success, but they baulked at her proposal that she invoke Belisama and they ask her for help.

"You don't know what the Gods are like," exclaimed Herla, "their cruel and capricious natures."

She raised an eyebrow in his direction. "Well, considering the fact that my goddess intervened when she thought I was going to burn out, she can't all be bad. Besides, I don't exactly have an option." Even now her hands itched to pick up her hammer and continue crafting. "I'm going to have to continue with my work for her; I don't have a choice."

Aerten went white. "A compulsion?"

She nodded. "It's not the end of the world; the compulsion ends when I finish this project for her and Leofric—the Ancient dragon that lives under the Downs—had an idea."

Their words rang once more in her mind. *There was power in the Hunt; if you could somehow harness the potential of their freedom, that would probably keep you stable whilst you finish your work.* But she didn't know how to explain it without sounding like she wanted to take advantage of them the way that Nodens had been for all these years.

"We should listen to the Ancient." It was the first words that Sten had spoken since she'd met him, and she had the feeling that what he said kind of went with the rest of the Hunt. He had a gravitas to him that radiated calm and decisiveness.

Morcant slipped his hand in hers, as if sensing her unease. "What did they say?"

"Something about harnessing the potential of your freedom to keep me stabilised whilst I work."

"To keep you stabilised so that the compulsion doesn't burn you up?"

"In both senses of the word, yes."

There was quiet whilst they all pondered this.

"Might I," asked Rina quietly, "make a suggestion?" There were no objections, and so she continued, "It would appear that you, the Hunt, are in a position of power here. Nodens wants to stop Kenna, and Belisama wants Kenna to keep going. Why don't you align yourselves with the goddess in exchange for a boon? I can help you phrase it in such a manner that leaves no room for doubt."

Herla nodded slowly, cautiously taking the lead for the Hunt. "That certainly has promise. And you would do this for us?"

"I'd do it for Kenna," said Rina, and Kenna was flooded with affection for her friend. Both Rina and Arlee had taken on this whole nightmare with barely a moment's hesitation, ready to charge forth for her, and she didn't know how to thank them.

"Stop it," Arlee said quietly, nudging her shoulder with theirs. "You know you'd do the same for us. No need to make a big deal."

She nodded. "This seems like it might work, and it would appear to be our only option, so I don't really think we have much choice."

Herla looked from her to Morcant and nodded slowly. "Then I suppose we should summon the goddess."

CHAPTER 22

"SO many mortals standing before me." Belisama's voice echoed around the forge and saw those that were strange to her flinch. "And some who seem to be standing centuries after they should have been buried. How very curious."

"We are the Hunt," *said one, only the slightest of tremors in his voice,* "Once wild and now freed."

Her flaming robes flared, and she was gratified to see that all of the Hunt took a nervous step backwards. None of this answering back from those who'd experienced the power the Gods first hand. "The Wild Hunt? And what, pray are you doing here?"

"Nodens trapped us for millennia, and then set us free only so that we could interfere with your plans. He demanded that we stop your priestess. We have come to you," *he added quickly, as one tendril of flame unfurled from her and began to reach out to him,* "because we know that on our own, we are unlikely to succeed."

The quiet that fell across the forge was eerie, and Belisama struggled to contain her anger, the flames that surrounded her pulsing with each breath she took. Nodens was not here. Had not been anywhere near here in centuries, and she knew that because he'd been trapped behind the veil, just as she had been before her priestess had awakened her. No, there was a far more dangerous deity in play. The person who'd attacked her, her, *with shadows when they could have embraced the night together.*

"I can assure you, Hunters, that Nodens has been as far from this place as a God can be. No, it has been that traitorous Belenus that has had you trapped all this time."

"What?" *One of them stepped forward in confusion.* "But he spoke to me, he *told* me—"

"You dare challenge me?" she demanded and was surprised as her priestess stepped forward to stand by the outspoken one's side. "You know not what I do. What I have seen. What he can do. You think that my compulsion is terrifying? Just wait until the Sun itself casts its fiery glance in your direction."

Although now she came to think about it, there hadn't been much light about Belenus when he'd been in her priestess's forge last; he'd been all shadows, and for a moment it saddened her, that his power had been twisted in such a manner.

Once it had been the both of them, ruling over flames and light and celebrations, sharing in the other's strengths, but he'd been conspicuously absent when they'd all been flung from this world behind the veil.

She had felt so alone, waiting—almost praying—for one touched by her priesthood to call out to her. So alone. And Belenus, her one-time companion, the Sun God to her Goddess of Fire, had been nowhere to be seen. She'd heard the calls to him though, the lighting of fire and dancing and drinking of mead as mortals celebrated Beltane, but she'd never gotten her share of worship, all of that energy spirited away elsewhere.

She felt it now, felt the strings tying her to the mortals standing before her. He'd used their power, the energy of their frozen lives, to lock her away so he could siphon off her power for himself. In taking on the mantle of Nodens and forcing the Wild Hunt to ride for centuries in a never-ending cycle, he had trapped her. And they? They had been as trapped as she.

A cry of anguish and pain that sent flames and smoke billowing upwards burst from her, and the sound tore at her very soul. This betrayal was almost too much to bear but bear it she would until she had her revenge.

And have revenge she would, even if it tore the sun itself out of the sky.

She turned to Kenna, her priestess, and ignored those who cowered beside her. For her priestess looked barely surprised, let alone shaken. "All I wanted was a way back in to the world; a path through your work. And not only has he intentionally kept me from my power for all this time, but he dared to try and destroy you too? Why should I not turn his Hunt to my advantage?"

The redheaded woman was calm as she spoke, but there was a steely determination in her Belisama recognised as her own metallic core. "They are just as much victims as you, your goddessness, and besides, without their help, I doubt I will survive the remainder of the compulsion."

She saw it then, their plan. To wrest the power of the Hunt away from Belenus, and to feed it through her priestess, to keep her strong enough to withstand the last of her forging.

"They will never be able to go back after," she warned. "Such power would indeed keep you alive, but once you let it go, it is gone forever. They would be stuck here."

"You mean," *said the warrior woman, whose face had been downcast for most of this interaction,* "that we could settle here? Make it our own?"

"If my priestess makes it through the final forging, then yes."

Another of the mortals stepped forward, one that she vaguely recognised from the last time she had been in the forge. This one had what appeared to be a board, with a document attached. "If we could perhaps get some assurances from your"—*she looked at*

Kenna briefly—"goddessness, about what the Hunt would be entitled to if they achieve this objective."

She laughed. They never failed to entertain, these tiny people, with their unshakeable belief in themselves. "What they would be entitled to? You mean as a boon?"

"As a pact."

"A pact..." She hadn't made a pact since she was last let loose on this world. She hadn't needed to with her priestess because priestesses barely needed much persuading about that kind of thing. But a pact would mean that the Hunt were bound to her as much as she was to them until it was complete. And it would make wresting control of them from that coward Belenus far easier. "What would my side of the pact be?"

"Once the forging is complete and Kenna is free of the compulsion, you will grant them a backstory. A history, if you will. Full lives as if they'd been born in the same age as us. A home, money, and the opportunities for them to get work as mortals and settle in this world. With us."

Paperwork. She hated the sound of that. The benefit of having an oral tradition of ritual, whether through Druids or priestesses, had been the fact that no one ever really needed anything written down. Her displeasure must have shown on her face though because the mortal added, "I can, of course, draw all of that up for you; it would just need your spark to bring it into existence."

That seemed fair, she supposed. "What of you?" The question was posed to Kenna who looked a little startled.

"Me?"

"When all of this is done and the compulsion is no longer, will you abandon me too?"

"That was an option?" *muttered one of the members of the Hunt, whose words were quelled when she turned her gaze on them.*

Her priestess didn't answer right away, pausing and looking about her. "I hadn't really thought about after," *she murmured, almost as if to herself.* "And I love flying, I don't want to lose my ability to shift."

She was so protective of the mortal, in a way that she never had with her priests and priestesses of old. Perhaps it had something to do with the fact that she'd been on her own for so long, starved of worship and prayer, but the more she looked at Kenna's face, the more she realised that she liked the woman. She was smart and skilful and didn't shy away from speaking her mind. Even back when Belisama had had sacrifices offered to her on a daily basis, she'd never interacted with mortals who weren't permanently terrified of her, and she found herself not wanting to lose that now.

"I had no intention of taking away your gifts," she said. "You were graced with them because you had earned them with your skill, and if you complete the task in front of you, you will have earned them many times over, so no. They are yours. But perhaps we could meet on less formal terms?"

It made her itch, talking like this in front of the other mortals, the ones who weren't of her ministry. But Belisama realised now that it was important to her to have at least one mortal who remembered her. "I could watch you work, once in a while."

"No compulsions?"

"No compulsions."

"And the pact with the Hunt?"

"That would also stand."

The smith nodded then and grinned suddenly. "Having a goddess, *The* Goddess of the Forge and Flame, as a patron would be pretty cool. And I could pick your brains about all kinds of ancient forging techniques. Yeah, I could do that."

She watched as the woman grabbed a knife from off her workbench and made a cut with the blade across her palm. Blood dripped down onto the head of the hammer that lay on the anvil, then Kenna handed it to the member of the Hunt who'd been at her side like a shadow. One by one they cut their palms, adding their own blood.

"I'm not giving you my blood," she said, not sure whether to be amused or angry at the prospect.

"I wouldn't ask you to. But your flame?"

And she understood then. Intermingled blood, heated with sacred fire, becoming one with the metal of the tool her priestess used. This would be Kenna's protection and would forge the Hunt together, closer than they had ever been. And blood magic was strong. It hadn't been used to forge their original bond, or she'd have been able to sense it. This would wrest them back from Belenus, and he would rue the day he crossed her.

CHAPTER 23

HE was so damn proud of her, his fȳr.

Her control of her fire, her skill in the forge, and her clear delight in what she did; she'd sacrificed none of that in her dealings with the goddess. She'd stood her ground, and even he could see that there was something akin to affection in Belisama's dealing with her. But there was still fear. He'd seen what Nodens—no, *Belenus*—could do, and the last thing he wanted was to lose her to *that.*

Morcant felt that fear creep back over him again. He would sacrifice himself if he must, anything to allow his fȳr to leave free of the shadows that had haunted him all this time.

Almost as if she could sense his concern, she walked over to him before starting her work, leading him slightly to the side so the others couldn't hear them.

"I'll be okay, I promise. I have all of you looking out for me, and so much time for us together when this is all over."

Time together. The words hit him harder than the fear, and he stared at her, confounded.

"Oh, Morcant." She laughed and kissed him with a smiling

mouth that felt like joy. "You said I love you; I thought you wanted us to—"

"Yes. Yes!" He seemed unable to say anything but yes as he pulled her close and kissed her back. "A thousand times yes, fȳr." He trusted in her, in them, and somehow just knew it would come out okay.

But when her newly reforged hammer hit the copper, Morcant felt it. He felt it in the very depths of his bones and, turning to look at the rest of the Hunt, he realised that they felt it too. That thrum in their veins echoing the sonorous hum left by the vibrations of the hammer against copper. They'd all stared at her for far too long, before she glared at them, and Arlee hurriedly moved them out the way.

"It's not a great idea to interrupt Kenna whilst she's forging at the best of times, let alone when there's sumat like this compulsion on her." They'd somehow rustled up chairs and big warming mugs of hot chocolate because Arlee declared that with all the bloodletting, they were worried about the effect on the Hunt's blood sugar.

Rina had taken to typing furiously at some machine in Kenna's office, only surfacing now and then to demand to know what they'd like to do with the rest of their lives. After being stared at blankly for a while, she'd rattled off a list of options before Arlee got her to slow down and really explain it.

"I need to get a work history written out for you all before all of this is done, and we don't know when your psycho god is going to turn up, so think fast."

Morcant had already thought about what he wanted. Years of standing by the sea, hearing it calling to him... He didn't want to fish on the waters, but he did want to spend time out there, and so Rina suggested the lifeguards. Sten had just said, "Horses," in that gruff final way of his, so that was him sorted, and Herla seemed determined to take on the most physical job possible, despite the fact that he didn't have all that much experience of anything outside hunting and politics. Groundskeeper or caretaker, Rina had decided, physical enough to satisfy whatever stubborn idea he had in his head, whilst also being close to nature. Deuroc wanted farmwork, and Aerten wanted to be a warrior.

"Unless you want to join the army and travel all over, there's not much call for warriors in this part of the world," Rina said ruefully.

"Wait! How about security work?" Arlee interjected. "Working in bars, throwing out unruly patrons and stepping in if someone is harassing someone else."

"Yes," said Aerten. "Write that down."

Rina looked at her from over the top of her glasses. "I beg your pardon?"

"Please?" The word was thrown away, but Aerten had softened her voice, so despite sighing and looking askance at the warrior woman, Rina wrote it down nonetheless.

"What are we to do now?" Herla had risen from his chair and was now pacing up and down. "We're just supposed to sit and wait for Belenus to turn up? And when he does, what are *we* supposed to do against him?"

"We fight," said Sten. He stood and nodded towards the workbench. "With tools."

THERE WAS A HUM OF ACTIVITY IN THE FORGE THAT reminded Morcant of centuries gone by, the sounds of a community at work together. They definitely felt like a community together, the Hunt and the Godsouched—and Arlee—all working towards the same common goal.

"Cazzo!" The curse was bitten out by Rina, but before her lips could close over the vowel, he saw Aerten stride across the forge with barely contained fury.

"What the fuck did you just say?" She was almost shaking with restrained fury, and the tension almost made him drop his hammer to the floor. Not now. Aerten couldn't do this now, not when there was so much else at stake.

Rina stood, slowly, and enunciated the word right in her face. "Cazzo. I said, 'cazzo'. Why? Got a problem with it?"

Deuroc, being closer to the women, tried to intercede, but Aerten shoved him off and stared blankly at the other woman. There was a pause in which all members of the Hunt held their breath. Aerten truly was a warrior, and if she unleashed her fury in the wrong direction…

Rina's voice softened. "Aerten, I didn't mean to…" She turned to look at Deuroc. "I don't know what I did?"

"I don't like Latin," Aerten bit out. "The fucking Romans —" Her words cut off, and Morcant let out a sigh of relief as she visibly shook her head and regained control of her emotions. "It's fine; I just didn't expect… My apologies."

The situation diffused, Morcant returned his focus to where Arlee was stood, musing over the table of weapons. "Have you used a weapon before?"

They grinned at him, all unrelenting cheerfulness. "I mean, my tongue can be pretty sharp… but no. Not really."

He smiled at them. "Do you like the look of any of these?"

Arlee grabbed at a broadsword and almost dropped it on their foot. "Fuck!"

"Perhaps something less pointy and heavy and more…"

"Something more manageable for the tiny enby?" They laughed. "That's probably a good idea. What would you suggest?"

He helped them pick out a couple of smaller daggers, before wandering over to where Kenna was forging. She was so consumed by her work but, when he dropped a kiss on her shoulder, she smiled vaguely.

"You!"

Nodens—no, Belenus—filled the doorway of the forge, disrupting their brief moment of serenity. Disrupting Morcant's happiness and kiss with a single word. He looked behind him to where Kenna stood at her anvil, fiercely forging, oblivious to the danger she faced. Good. He didn't want her to worry when he did what had to be done.

Stepping forward, he breathed in slowly, trying to summon courage from whatever reserves he had, and face the god head on.

"You dare defy me?" Belenus's words crept across his skin. There was no shouting now, just a quiet rage that crawled through the forge, shadows enveloping every surface. Darkness pushed at the edge of his mind, and Morcant almost staggered.

This was too much. *Too much.* He could not bear it alone. He could not save the Hunt, and he could not save Kenna, and he could not escape his fate.

But a heavy hand landed on his shoulder, and he turned to see Herla next to him, dark hair about his face. "You are not alone, Morcant. You are of the Hunt."

Then the hot rush of blood swept through his veins, bringing echoes of the other members of the Wild Hunt with it, each of them strong and steady. With him always. And then, there at the back, a wave of heat that he knew was Kenna. They were in this together.

As one, the Hunt stepped towards Belenus, and when Herla spoke, it held all the power that they'd fused together. "This isn't defiance. This is revenge."

They were the Hunt, breaking free of *his* confines, and they were ready to fight.

⚔⚔⚔

KENNA HAD MANAGED TO SHUT OUT ALL OF THE TALK AND the sounds behind her as she worked, focusing on heating and sculpting the metal into shape until she completed each ray of light. Copper hardened by hammering, heated to smooth blemishes, and cooled with water.

There was a clang behind her and a "fuck yeah!" that sounded suspiciously like Arlee. She dreaded to think what was going to happen now that bouncy, overly enthusiastic Arlee had their hands on some kind of weapon. Hopefully they'd make it through the melee without knocking themselves out with it.

Kenna took a breath and looked at the completed rays before her, ready to move on to affixing them to the main sculpture when she saw it out of the corner of her eye. A shadow.

She longed to take her hammer and swing at it, the way she had the first time, but this time she knew she had to trust in the others. Trust in their ability to keep her safe as she worked, until they could all be done with this. But she knew the wandering, faceless shapes of smoke and shadow were there now, meandering all over her forge, and it fuelled her almost more than the compulsion was.

As she shoved the handle of her hammer into her belt and turned to gather all the copper, she caught sight of the scene behind her.

The shadowgod was back—Belenus she supposed—and with him more of those awful, draining shadows, that swirled round each and every nook and cranny of her forge. And there was a coldness in the air that was just wrong, especially now that she knew that he was a Sun God. A Sun God should be joyous; filling up a space with warmth and delight, but there was none of that now; her forge was cold and hard, and she itched to fill it with her own flames, to rush into combat with him herself, and wipe that complacent look from his face with a swing of her hammer.

But she couldn't. She had work to do.

The Hunt had formed a protective semicircle around her and the statue so she could do that work, and as she turned her head to look at them, everything felt like it was slowing down, like that split second before you spill a cup of tea or fall over. An inevitability in the air made her want to cry.

They were facing off against an onslaught of darkness that seemed to creep ever closer, attempting to meet each tendril of shadow with a clash of metal. Sten with long methodical swings, Deuroc with short jabs, and Herla wielding the practice sword that she'd forged for a larper who'd never collected it. She could see the outline of Rina was still typing in the office, door guarded by Aerten, who was whirling metal around like a woman possessed. Even the Hound was snapping at any shadows he could reach. And Morcant? Morcant was so close to her she could have reached out to touch him, had she so wanted.

Almost as if he could hear her thoughts, he threw a look over his shoulder, sweat pouring down his face. "You're alright, fȳr?"

She went to nod, averting her eyes from where the darkness seemed to be closing in and turned until she saw him, Belenus, staring at her.

"Kenna?"

That complacent look was aimed at her now, and something tugged at the very core of her, at that place where she instinctively knew that her fire dwelt.

"Kenna!"

She jerked back to look at Morcant, taking in a jagged breath that felt cold right down to her toes.

"Perhaps a little more forging, please…" He gestured with

his free hand at the statue behind her, and it jolted her into action.

Kenna strode hurriedly over to the statue, each step shoring her up, taking her closer to completion. All she had to do now was to affix the rays to the sculpture.

A huff of laughter. All she had to do; there was nothing easy about this last step of the project. All the forging and casting and hammering, that was the easy part. Pulling it all together would challenge her skills as blacksmith under normal circumstances. And under these…

Stepping up to the figure, she ran her hands over metal that felt cool beneath her hands, and everything else faded away once more. Clangs melted into silence, and there was just her and her work.

She was working with three very different types of metal—steel, bronze, and now copper—each with a different heating point. Trying to affix the copper rays with bolts, the way she had with the steel flames, just seemed like cheating. And she didn't want to cheat. She couldn't cheat.

It had to be fire.

Picking up the first ray, she knew exactly where it had to go. Round the back of the figure so that the woman before her would not just be rising up out of flames, she would be made of flames. Kenna could see it. Physically see it on the statue in front of her, as if someone had overlayed an image of where each ray would go. The image was alight in her mind's eye, and even when she blinked, it was there, scorched onto her retinas.

It would be a delicate operation. Heating, then hammering, and then reheating. And if she overdid the flames or the fall of her hammer even the slightest, the figure beneath the rays would be ruined. Fuck.

CHAPTER 24

ALL around him was heat and shadows and anger.

Morcant cast aside another shadow with a swing of the double-headed hammer that he'd selected from the tools on Kenna's workbench. The shadows were coming all the quicker now, almost overwhelmingly so, and behind them he could see Belenus inching ever closer. One step at a time. Those eyes, taunting him, as if to say 'Why would now be any different?' Why would today be the day they'd break free of his grasp, when centuries of entrapment proved otherwise?

He'd chosen to stand his ground beside Kenna, beside his fȳr, because he needed to be her last defence against that god, that *thing*, that had tortured him for two millennia. In theory, perhaps one of the other members of the Hunt, one with more fighting experience, should have taken up that last-stand post, but no one had challenged him. None of them would be more motivated than he to fight to the death for his Kenna.

A grunt from where Aerten had also taken up a protective stance, perhaps out of guilt for how she'd reacted to Rina's words earlier, made him glance over. Her eyes met his, ablaze. It was so easy to forget how many of the others had lived through the heat of battle. Clashes of swords, hammer meeting flesh, and the frenzied rage that came with the determination to protect one's own. Alongside her mother and sister, Aerten had led men to bring cities to their very knees. Sten had been the last man standing in a battle that was enshrined in legend even to this day, and Deuroc and Herla had fought side by side many a time.

But today they all looked wearied after only a short time fighting.

He might have had the least experience of the five of them, but he had passion. And anger. He was so damn angry. And that raw fury? It swept through his veins.

If he hadn't been protecting Kenna, he wasn't sure whether he would be able to stop himself from charging straight at Belenus. The god had lied to him for centuries; had tortured him and his friends; had made their lives pieces in a game played by creatures who couldn't possibly grasp the preciousness of a mortal life lived well and to its fullest.

He hated him.

Morcant would die before he let Belenus achieve his end goal, but he didn't want that. He wanted to live. He wanted revenge, and that revenge would be threefold. It would be the joy of living out the brevity of a mortal life beside his Kenna. It would be the satisfaction of knowing—seeing—his friends, his family, freed from the constraints of the Hunt for good. And it would be the cold hard gratification of seeing the god's plans all disintegrate into nothingness, just as his brother had.

All they had to do was to hold the line. To keep the shadows that tried to cling to any and all surfaces, from Kenna. To make sure that nothing could stop her from saving them all from a never-ending life unblemished by the vitality of true existence.

⚒⚒⚒

AS SHE LET THE FINAL FLAMES ON HER BREATH DIE DOWN, Kenna felt the compulsion fall away from her as if she were shedding her scales. Tears fell, unbidden, down her cheeks and she took in ragged breaths, each one deeper and longer than the last.

The bubble of silence she'd been suspended in burst, and sound flooded in, knocking her off her feet until she found herself kneeling at the foot of the statue, holding on to the flames, as if to grasp at something of the drive that had just left her.

They warmed beneath her hands, and when they flared into existence, her skin seemed immune to their warmth. Then there were flaming fingers beneath her chin, nudging her face up until she looked into Belisama's eyes. The goddess was glorious, and she wasn't just wearing the flames this time, she was aflame.

Somehow, she knew that if she'd been anyone else gazing upon this might of power, it would have been too much to bear. But she wasn't anyone else; she was Kenna. Blacksmith. Dragon. Priestess. And she'd offered so much of herself, of her energy, to Belisama that the power she saw in the goddess's face had a touch of her own art about it.

Tiny sparks broke away from the goddess's flames and chased the tears from Kenna's face. *"Of all my priestesses,"* she said, her words quiet, just for the two of them, *"You will always be the one I love the most."*

Kenna felt a calming sensation then, as the goddess stepped forward, and raised a single hand. It flooded through her veins, slowing her heartbeat and regulating each breath until she was almost floating. Even turning her head felt sluggish, and when she looked across her forge, everyone else seemed suspended in time too, their movements slowing to a crawl.

Belisama took a breath and when she blew outward, as if to blow away a cobweb, the gust caught the shadows, tearing them asunder, ripping them from corners and under tables, leaving small patches of nothingness where they'd clung to walls.

The goddess kept a hold of Kenna until she reached Morcant. There, she turned her stare on the man with such intensity that Kenna was surprised that he didn't immediately wither beneath it.

"One day you may be worthy of her."

His smile then, was one of understanding. "And until that day, I'll do my best."

She felt the touch of Belisama's lips on her brow, a kiss that flared before sinking beneath her skin until she could feel it all over. Then Morcant took her in his arms, each movement slow and deliberate. Enveloping her with such tenderness that this time, when she cried, it was from relief. Relief from being free of that overwhelming compulsion to work, free from the torment that had driven her goddess, and relief that she could finally stand here and let go because she had Morcant. Because he had her.

But still she watched, tears notwithstanding, as Belisama met Belenus in the centre of the forge.

The shadows that had been about the god's face had been dispersed , but the brightness of his visage seemed somewhat faded in comparison to her goddess's. There was frustration and anger, but also tiredness, and when Belisama held out her hand for his, he seemed almost hopeful.

"I've been waiting for you, for so long."

"Lie." There was a tone in the goddess's voice that Kenna had never heard before. It was sharp and grating, like a metal point dragged across a file, and she shuddered. *"Betrayer."*

His face transformed then, ugly, and Morcant's arms tightened about her involuntarily. So this was the deity that he'd had to deal with, time after time. This was the face of the god who'd almost destroyed her Morcant. And she wanted to scream obscenity after obscenity at him, to beat him down until he felt a fraction of the torment that the man who cared for her had.

In one swift movement, Belenus thrust out his arm and said, *"To me, my Hunt,"* and she started as the hammer tucked into her belt, hummed and then jolted upwards and away.

She tried to grab it, but it was too fast for her, practically zooming across the forge until one flaming hand plucked it from the air. Kenna trembled then. Her blood was in the hammer; she could feel it, as she was certain that all the members of the Hunt could also feel it. Calling to her. To them.

The metal head of the hammer strained in a manner that she'd never seen metal move before. As Belisama brought it crashing to the ground, shattering the head into a million pieces, she screamed. And when she screamed, it felt as though the whole world was screaming with her.

It was awful. Unbearable. It brought tears to her eyes, and she wanted to curl up in a corner and shut out the terrible, terrible sound.

It was the kind of sound that stuck, buried beneath your skin, and clung there. She knew, in that moment, that she would never be able to unhear it. That it would return to her dreams again and again, and she found herself trembling with untold grief.

And then, just as suddenly as it had started, it stopped.

She felt drugged, as if she were moving in slow motion,

and it wasn't until Morcant stumbled towards her, his hands reaching out to help her to her feet, that she had a chance to look around. The members of the Wild Hunt, slowly getting to their feet, the Hound by their feet, tail wagging, jumping up to lick hands. They looked as dazed as she felt, but they were safe.

Oh, so it had all turned out okay then?

It didn't feel okay though. The shadows may have been gone from the forge, but *he* wasn't. Not yet.

The Hunt was free, she could feel that as clearly as if she'd wrenched their magical chains from his grasp herself, and now Belisama was bent on her revenge.

Tendrils of flames encircled the shadowgod, flaring until he was forced to his knees. He was dragged across the floor to where Belisama stood, deep scorch marks in his wake. Kenna somehow knew that they'd never fade, her forge always scarred by Belenus's downfall.

But his eyes, there was nothing but cold hatred. Hatred for all of them, but most of all for the goddess who held his fate in her hands and in her flames.

Belisama stood there for a long time, a deep sorrow flashing across her face, looking down at the god who'd betrayed her. Then a twist of her hand, and he was gone. Banished into some other realm that Kenna didn't care to think of.

MORCANT WAS FAIRLY CERTAIN THAT HE WANTED THE NEXT few days to consist of very little other than kissing Kenna. There was likely to be practicalities that the rest of the Hunt and Rina would want to talk through, but in his mind, nothing took precedent over this. Over her.

"You were magnificent, fȳr."

She laughed, a gurgled that rippled up until she was laughing in his arms. "I was forging; you guys were the ones who kept me alive, who made it happen."

"A joint effort then," he answered, settling his hands about her waist, even as hers joined around his neck.

"A joint effort." Her smile was warming. Not in that overwhelming spark of fire that lay between them so often, but like the fire in the hearth, heating an entire room.

She was like that.

Them *together* made him feel like that. And as all-consuming as those raging flames could be, this was the fire that he wanted for the rest of his mortal life.

"I love you." He'd said it before, but this time the words were drawn from his soul. Previously he'd meant it, had believed it, but in that transient place where he didn't know if he were free of the Hunt, there'd been a sorrowfulness in them that had almost broken him. Now, freed from the Hunt, they felt full of hope and possibilities.

She looked up, her eyes searching for something in his and then a small secret smile crossed her face as she huffed out a tiny laugh. "It seems so unreal, doesn't it? Loving someone this much."

His heart stuttered in a manner not unsimilar to when the curse of the Hunt had been wrenched from them. "What?"

"I love you too. Of course, I do." And then she was kissing him again and the fire between them flared into a comfortable glow.

EPILOGUE

✵✵✵

FROM beyond the veil, Andraste watched as Belenus was thrown back, beaten down and exhausted. He'd always been a little too pompous for her liking, and she'd never understood quite what Belisama saw in him, but with the power of ritual stripped away from him, he seemed nothing but a bitter old man.

She tuned out most of his ramblings until her ears alighted upon a single word. Godstouched.

She'd had her own Godstouched in her time. Women who'd fought furiously for her, who'd died to sate her need for battle, who'd driven men to the point of distraction. Whole cities had been razed to the ground in her name, and she missed it so.

So if there were Godstouched roaming the Earth, perhaps there would be one who'd be able to help her find what she needed. Be able to guide her back to what was once lost.

She wanted an Oracle, and by her godhead itself, if there was one now alive, she would have them.

ACKNOWLEDGMENTS

This world of the Freed Hunt has sat in my head now for nearly five years, and to finally be able to share it with you is a privilege that I wasn't sure would ever happen. It's the beginning of a series—and a universe—of gods and magic and shagging that's never been far from my thoughts. And once more I have oh so many people to thank.

Firstly, to my editor D. Ann Williams, for being kind with your critique, even as you made me a better writer. You are patient and talented and have a skill for drawing out exactly what a book most needs.

To Teresa of Wolfsparrow Covers, for this beautiful cover that I adore. It's so gorgeous and fiery and exactly what I wanted! I can't wait for everyone to see the rest of the series' covers.

To Coralie Moss, for formatting this into something ready for publication, and for talking about goddesses with me.

I joined Wordmakers in January 2021, burnt out from the pandemic, and not sure that I would ever really be ready to write again, and I found my home. Thanks Tasha L. Harrison for founding this safe space, and thank you, oh so much, to the writers who make it such a great place to be: Rae Shawn, K.K.H., Mia Heintzelman, Karmen Lee, Fortune Whelan, Amanda Cinelli, Katee Robert, Meka James, Jordan Monroe, Jerica Taylor, Elysabeth Grace, and Lisa Kessler.

Thanks also go to Talia Hibbert, Eden Bradley, Stefanie Simpson, Aleksandr Voinov, Marie Lipscomb, Renée Dahlia,

Kait Gamble, Mina Waheed, Sonia Palermo, Holly March, Sarah E. Lily, and J. Emery, for being just the best writer friends I could ask for.

To my beta readers: Agata, Aleks, Cat, Kate, Matt, Rebecca, Rebel, Stef, Talia, Tara, and Teresa. You believed in this book before I really did myself, so thank you so much for that.

Special thanks to John Jacobson, who was the first person to show any interest in Kenna and Morcant.

Corey, here's your enby dragon, Leofric; I hope you love them.

And Oli, that denimed thigh line is for you, as promised.

To my wildly chaotic family whom I adore. To my parents, whose love for each other lights up every room that they're in; I hope my characters have HEAs as satisfying as yours has been. Thank you for being the best, most supportive parents a girl could ask for. To my siblings (in age order, to prevent scuffles): Lucia, you are always there to talk and nerd out with me, and my life is so enriched by having you in it. Fran, my passionate, activist sister; your determination to change the world makes me want to do the same. Dom, thank you for never being too cool to hang out with your older sister, even though you are most definitely the coolest of us all.

To my grandparents: Gran, for showing me what a strong, independent woman looks like, and for loving us fiercely. Nonno, I've inherited your love language, and I promise to always cook for those I love, just as you have for me. And Nanna, I think you'd be so proud of all I've accomplished; I miss you every day.

To N. From the moment you met me, you believed in me, in my writing, and in all I could accomplish. Thank you for your kindness, your silliness, and your love. The world seems that much brighter when I'm with you, and the life we've built together brings me so much joy. Lubs.

And finally (yes, I'm nearly done), to you dear reader, for picking up this book and giving it a try. Thank you for making my dreams come true.

ABOUT ALI

Ali Williams' inner romance reader is never quite satisfied, which is why she oscillates between writing romance, editing romance, and studying it as part of her PhD.

She can be found at the foot of the South Downs in the UK, either nerding out over local mythologies, reading tarot cards, or making homemade pasta, according to her Nanna's recipes.

She believes with all of her bifurious heart that writing romance is an act of rebellion and that academia will be so much better when studying diverse HEAs is naturally part of the curriculum.

Follow Ali on:

Twitter | Facebook | Instagram | TikTok

Lightning Source UK Ltd.
Milton Keynes UK
UKHW010735160522
403059UK00003B/154